Louisa had no illusions about her own appeal to the heart of a man like Lord Geffrey. With his handsome person, respected title, and considerable wealth, he could choose any woman of rank for his wife. Certainly a wife of beauty and elegance would be his first choice. Any love that Louisa felt for him would never be returned.

She thought long and hard about her future. Unrequited love was a most unhappy state of feeling to look forward to.

But Louisa was in for a surprise....

Also by Sarah Carlisle:

WIDOW AUBREY

Cleopatra's Carpet

SARAH CARLISLE

FAWCETT COVENTRY • NEW YORK

CLEOPATRA'S CARPET

Published by Fawcett Coventry Books, a unit of CBS Publications, the Consumer Publishing Division of CBS Inc.

ISBN: 0-449-50009-8

Printed in the United States of America

First Fawcett Coventry printing: December 1979

10 9 8 7 6 5 4 3 2 1

I

"How dare you treat me like this!" Lady Melinda Whitworth stormed angrily, the high color on her cheeks adding immensely to her beauty.

"Mel, damn it, be reasonable," Lord Geffrey answered tartly. "It's hardly unreasonable of me to attend to the affairs of my estates." He was very angry with the young woman before him, resenting her peevish demands on him despite her undoubted beauty.

Lady Melinda Whitworth was the daughter of an earl, an heiress with a sizeable dowry, and acclaimed beauty to boot. Her silvery blond hair was swept up into a pile of curls on her head, a scattering of tiny diamond flowers twinkling among the soft strands that were beginning to go astray as she shook her head with anger. A delightful mouth, creamy complexion, and a figure unusually well rounded for one who was only seventeen, all had led her to an intoxicating success in her first Season. She was accustomed to men worshiping at her feet, and more. Willie Swinnerton had pledged eternal love and expressed it with the gift of a dozen hothouse orchids every day. Edward Roche had practically camped out in Park Lane, keeping her father's house in constant view whenever she was home. Lord Feld had challenged poor Edward to a duel, claiming that Roche's attentions were unseemly and embarrassing to the young lady so honored. Melinda's father, the Earl of Whitworth, had squelched that plan quite handily, dryly commenting that a duel would bring even more scandal than that to his daughter's name. And Melinda, always a trifle spoiled, had adored every minute of it.

Showered with poems, poesies, delightful little notes, demands of marriage, love, even friendship as a last resort, Melinda had come to accept the notion that everyone should cater to her every whim, which they did in any case. And now Francis, Lord Geffrey, was claiming the pressure of mere business to excuse himself from tomorrow's lovely picnic. Melinda's soulful brown eyes filled with tears, her thick, sable lashes catching the first few drops as they fell.

Lord Geffrey looked at her apprehensively. He

had been a damned fool, at his age to become involved with a miss barely out of the school room. Dancers from the opera house were more his style, dancers put up expensively .in town houses and squired about in the finest carriages pulled by high-spirited teams. Or married ladies who were aware of the rules of the oh, so polite game called Love, and who could be relied upon to behave with discretion. Women who could be easily shrugged off.

What had turned his head? The soft innocence? The romantic beauty of the gardens, such as this, where the fountain murmured softly in the background, muffling their voices? The gentle looks that relied on neither paints nor powder for enhancement? Or simply the fact that Melinda had made none of the usual overt demands on him, never dreaming of dangling for an emerald necklace or a new matched team. For a few blessed weeks Francis Geffrey had felt at home with the Whitworth family. There had been an easy going hospitality that had appealed to his jaded tastes. And Melinda had been like a lovable little sister to him.

But now this! Was she going to demand more and more of his time and attention? His past affairs had ended when the relationship had reached that point. Or was she going to make the most important demand of all? Was she going to expect an offer of matrimony from an eligible bachelor who was old enough to know what he was about when

7

he spent such a marked amount of time in a young lady's company?

Oh, Lord! What the hell was he to do? He had probably compromised himself by now and would have the earl after him with a demand for marriage.

"I hate you, Francis Geffrey! You aren't a nice man at all, and I never want to speak to you again," Lady Melinda sobbed dramatically, her plump breasts heaving. When he failed to respond with more than a bemused look of amazement and a proffered handkerchief, she somewhat ruined her tragic pose by stamping her tiny foot on the ground and gasping at him, "Men! You are all horrible! Every single one of you! Only Edward understands me and deals kindly with me. I must find him at once!" And with this paradoxical statement she whirled around and began to sail, with dignity, out of the conservatory and toward the main part of the house, her chin up and her eyes suddenly dry.

Until she collided with another young lady who was coming around the fountain from the direction of the house.

"Oh, dear, Mel! So sorry, I wasn't watching where I was going," the other lady said apologetically as she stooped to fetch the fan that had fallen from Lady Melinda's hand to the ground in her agitation. "Whatever are you doing out here? George Menzies is searching high and low for you. You had promised him this dance."

"Georgie? Oh, I had forgotten all about him! At least *he* knows how to be a good friend," and having cast an angry glance over her shoulder at Lord Geffrey, she swept up the hall toward the brightly lit ballroom.

"Oh, dear!" Miss Louisa Bardoff whispered in dismay. "I seem to have walked into something, haven't I?" she asked anxiously of Lord Geffrey. Then catching sight of his angry face as he hastily stuffed his rejected handkerchief into his pocket, she became even more flustered

"I just didn't see you here, in the dark, and I didn't hear you here because of the fountain," she stammered. Lord Geffrey continued to look very stiff and proper, avoiding her eyes.

"I only came out for a rest, you see. All this practicing has quite worn me out."

Lord Geffrey looked confused. "Practicing?"

Heartened by the sudden humanization of his manner, Miss Bardoff babbled on. "Oh, yes. I am to be shot off this next Season and Papa says that I ought to learn my way around a bit first. He says that it will be ever so much more fun that way. So I am meeting people at house parties like this one. He says it is very important."

The tall, imposing man before her was suddenly cool again. "Yes meeting eligible bachelors is of prime consideration, Miss, uh, Miss . . . ?" he hinted with hauteur. "I don't believe that I have had the honor of being presented to you."

"Bardoff. Miss Louisa Bardoff. My papa is Sir Harry Bardoff of Bardoff Hall. And you are Lord Geffrey," she smiled back.

"At your service, Miss Bardoff," Geffrey said sardonically. Then he added a flourishing bow as an afterthought.

Miss Bardoff's eyes gleamed a moment, then she dipped into a most proper curtsey.

"Actually, I already know lots of people. Melinda, for example. We used to play together quite a bit. She is only a few months older than I. And I know her brothers, and friends of my brother and my Colville cousins."

"Then you aren't searching for a husband, Miss Bardoff?" he asked with calm amazement.

"Husband?" Miss Bardoff looked at him with equal amazement. "Oh, heavens, no! I already have one, you see!"

"You are married then, ah, *Miss* Bardoff?"

"Oh, no. Just betrothed. To Tommy Colville, my cousin. Second cousin, actually."

By now Lord Geffrey's sense of humor was taking over as he tried to sort his way through this unusual conversation he was in. His companion was proving to be full of surprises and not uninteresting.

"Then why bother with a Season? I thought the whole idea was for a young lady to seek a suitable husband. Is there something more to it that I am not aware of?"

"Oh, of course! After all, my lord, many people of the *Ton* are already married!"

"True. But they all still seem to be seeking," he said wrily.

Miss Bardoff looked momentarily confused, then her face lit up. "You must mean people such as Mrs. Hay. She certainly *is* seeking," she giggled. "My mama won't let me talk to her, not at all. Not that the lady wants to talk to *me!*"

For the first time in many years, Lord Geffrey was at a loss for words. This plump young girl with her round, girlish figure and gray eyes, who reminded him somewhat of a mourning dove in the dim light, seemed to combine a remarkable degree of innocence and sophistication. She was pressing on, unembarrassed by a topic of conversation that would certainly not meet with her mother's approval. He should never have spoken so in her presence.

"Papa says that I must meet other people. The great ladies, and old family friends and acquaintances whom I have not seen in years. And learn how to dress properly and be a gracious guest and dance in really big balls, not just the small ones we have sometimes in the neighborhood. And Mama will begin putting me in the way of running a London household. Tommy's family has a town house, you know, and some day he will inherit the title and it is important that I know how to do things properly. Don't you agree?"

"Very creditable," he murmured uncomfortably as the rush of words momentarily halted. His impulse to laugh was growing to be very nearly uncontrollable and he looked at her somewhat owlishly as he strove to stifle it.

"I also think that Papa wants me to have a bit of fun before we are married, so that I won't feel that I missed anything afterward. That could be important, I suppose. After all, the match has been set since we were children. Some people might resent that."

Arrested, Geffrey looked at her with renewed interest. Sir Harry Bardoff would appear to be a shrewd man, in her alloted role in life, and Miss Bardoff would seem to have inherited some of that shrewdness.

"Then you are to be envied, Miss Bardoff. You may enjoy the coming Season without worry, for the most difficult and important task of your entire life has already been attended to by loving parents. I congratulate you!" he ended humorously.

"Do you mean finding a husband?" she asked with glee. "Is that your idea of what is difficult and important?"

"It is many women's idea of importance," he answered with a laugh.

Miss Bardoff looked pleased. "I am so glad you have finally laughed. You were looking like an owl a few moments ago. And you are much handsomer this way!"

By now Lord Geffrey was gasping for breath, the embarrassing scene of a few minutes before totally driven from his mind. This absurd girl, calling him an owl!

"And don't worry about Mel. She may sulk a bit, but she will get over it. And she wasn't really serious about you anyway."

His head snapped up, his pride offended.

"Then she was certainly giving a convincing performance," he replied dryly.

"Oh, no. I mean that she likes you quite a bit, but you are too . . . I mean that you are too serious and dignified for her. She is still rather a little girl."

"You are trying to tell me that I am too old for her!"

"Not at all. She was quite flattered by your attentions. You are very handsome, you know, and many ladies like you."

"And I suppose that the display of emotion that I was treated to this evening meant nothing?"

Miss Bardoff looked thoughtful. "I think that she had her heart set on the punting afterwards, although why she would want to at this time of year I can't imagine. Edward isn't very good at it, you know. Not at all."

Realizing that she had once again insulted him despite the best of intentions, she looked up at him with an embarrassed look on her face and tried to stammer another apology.

13

"There is no need for you to explain, Miss Bardoff. I quite understand what you mean," he said coldly.

"Oh, dear. I haven't expressed myself very well, not at all. Besides, you really don't care do you? I rather thought that you were getting nervous several times this evening."

"Louisa?" a young masculine voice suddenly called out. "Wherever are you? We must dance the waltz together and it is already started. Louisa? Do come!"

"Oh, dear. That's Ruston, my brother. More practice." And with that she slipped away behind the screen of water.

After she had left Lord Geffrey realized that he had forgotten to ask for her silence regarding the scene she had witnessed. Damnation! The chit would babble it to everyone at the party. Lady Mel would probably keep silent to protect her hurt pride that he had not come to heel. She was also a well brought up girl. But Miss Bardoff would undoubtedly enjoy spreading this juicy tidbit about.

Damn. It would be among all his friends in a matter of a few days. Those who weren't at the party would hear of it from the others. Well, at least he had already made his excuses to his hostess and could leave early tomorrow before he had his childish behavior thrown in his face. He would leave very early.

After the music ended young Mr. Ruston Bardoff returned his sister, Miss Bardoff, to their mother and sped off before his indulgent parent could quiz him on the progress of the dance.

Louisa smoothed her muslin skirts down, then seated herself next to Lady Marie. For a moment she admired the blue ribbons banding the lower edge of her skirt. When she was married she would be able to wear a whole dress of blue like that, and in a style of her own choosing. She was sure that this shade would bring out the blue flecks in her gray eyes.

"Well, dear. How did it go?" Lady Marie asked her eldest daughter kindly.

"Quite well, Mama. I think that I am better than Ruston at the waltz. I am now able to keep my toes out of the way of his boots."

Lady Marie chuckled. "I am glad to hear that. It will stand you in good stead."

"Yes. I thought that it would," her daughter agreed complacently.

"It is quite a daring thing, the waltz, but I am sure that Lady Cowper will allow you to dance it with Tommy when you appear at Almack's Assembly, so you must be ready."

"Yes, Mama," Louisa murmured. Her mind was already wandering to the prospect of supper. "That is the best way, undoubtedly. Shall we go down to the supper room? I promised Melinda that I would sit by her. We have so much to talk about, but she

15

has been quite busy dancing the whole of the evening."

"Very well, dear, run along and have a good gossip. I am not quite ready to go myself. And send that young Lord Geffrey over to me afterwards. I want to have a word with him about his mother."

"I believe that he has already left the dance floor, Mama," Louisa said indifferently.

"Oh? Strange. He was dangling around Mel so. But perhaps he plans to leave early in the morning. Such an impulsive young man."

But by then Louisa had turned away, anxious to put a certain good intention into effect.

II

Louisa's Season had been everything that she had hoped it to be. At least, the two weeks she had so far experienced had presented no surprises. There had been two balls, a reception, a Venetian breakfast, three dinners, a visit to Richmond Gardens (a somewhat chilly outing for late March), and naturally a theater party and an evening at the opera. After all, Lady Bardoff prided herself on her cultural interests.

The mild success was to be expected. To begin with, the Bardoffs, with their Colville and Sitwell connections, claimed as their right *entré* into the highest circles of the *Ton*. Sir Harry's notions of propriety might be a trifle old fashioned in that he

disdained most of the social climbers who had
found favor with Society by being merely amusing,
but in many quarters this did him no harm. Lady
Bardoff had been the youngest daughter of an earl,
and although she had married a mere baronet, her
father had seen to it that the bridegroom's fortune
was ample and that his family was of the first respectability. Equally important, Sir Harry was a
man of sense who was fond of his wife and toler-
ated her undoubted foolishness. And so Louisa
swirled through the great ballrooms and supped
with the noblest in the land, secure in her position
in Society.

Her mother, whose understanding was not at all
strong in practical matters, these being in the masculine province in her estimation, had an inbred
sense of what was right and proper in her own
milieu. Louisa was dressed unexceptionally, if a
trifle childishly, in sprigged muslin and laces and
flounces and cunning little bows provided by the
best modiste in town. The colors tended toward
pale pinks and yellows, with a cherry ribbon the
most vivid article in her toilette. That this style
made an already round figure rounder went uncom-
mented, and Louisa philosophically made the best
of it, appreciating that her mama was in many ways
the kindest, most generous and best of parents. After all, Lady Bardoff was bearing the expense of her
best friend's Season, something that Louisa deeply
appreciated.

Louisa's manners were declared pretty by the people who counted, those great hostesses and dowagers who issued invitations to all of the really important social gatherings. Under her mother's guidance, she dropped a curtsey to each of them, listened attentively to whatever they happened to be saying, and asked the proper questions (often hastily whispered into her ear by Lady Bardoff) about gowns, children, parties, weddings and mutual friends. Lady A's silk gloves were from Paris, smuggled in near her husband's estate in Kent, Mrs. M had recently arranged the engagement of her daughter to a man of rank but not fortune, Miss F's dress was charming indeed. Under her mother's guidance she was able to say the right word at the right moment, often with a spark of her own wit that her mother failed to notice but that the ladies found amusing.

And then, the knowledge that she was promised to Tommy Colville, a knowledge that was surprisingly common despite the lack of a formal announcement in the *Times*, caused the mamas among the hostesses to be even more cordial. Louisa posed no threat to the plainest daughter desperately searching for a husband, and was looked upon as a welcome addition to any party. Even the young men were more at ease around her, being able to put off the flirtatious affectations decreed by Society as being the proper mode of conduct when with a young lady. Louisa was a girl who wasn't the least bit interested in flirting, a fact sworn to by her brother's friends. She was safe to all concerned.

Papa had been right, for it was her father who had insisted that she have a Season, a fact swept aside by Mama in the bustle of perparations. It was a Season that she would cherish in her memories. That Louisa's own laughing disposition added immensely to her popularity she would never have credited. Although not a beauty, she had fine gray eyes that were always alight with laughter, and many young men privately thought that she was really quite a pretty little thing with her lovely brown hair and good complexion, and nice to have around to boot. She might not fit the current fashion of blondes, but no matter. The most callow youth could feel at ease around her and even unbend for a good laugh now and then, basking in the warmth of her tolerant approval. Louisa somehow brought out the best in most people.

It was a rare moment when Lord Geffrey came across her at Countess Saltire's ball, standing off to the side in the cool breeze of an open french window. She wasn't aware of his presence on the terrace outside, her attention being held by the swirl of dancers on the floor before her.

Geffrey debated speaking to her, unsure of how to approach her after their previous encounter. After all, he had not shown to advantage on the occasion and had even been somewhat gauche. This was the first ball he had attended since then, and he had steeled himself to face the mockery of his friends and acquaintances. The story of his infatuation with Lady Melinda and its attending tangles was too good for the *Ton* to ignore. But on this evening no amount of prevarication could withstand the demands of his widowed mother that he escort her to this important event, and with a gloomy countenance he had accepted the inevitable.

Much to his surprise, there had been no comment. Friends had railed him for his sudden hermit-like ways, but beyond that everything was as usual. Lady Melinda had nodded to him from across the room, a pleasant smile on her face, then turned back to a very attentive young guardsman. She had been cajoled into a better humor by her friend Louisa, and she had even quite forgiven him his rudeness, putting it down to mere stodginess.

So much for being the *on dit* of the Town, he thought ruefully. Unaware of the veil of secrecy that had been pulled across the event, he was even mildly piqued. It appeared that Lord Geffrey's actions weren't worthy of notice, even for the sake of laughter.

He was just beginning to feel at ease when he came across Louisa standing in the open window. Having cast his mind over the possible topics of conversation available to him, he had decided to make a discrete withdrawal. After all, the one thing that they had in common was the very thing that he wanted most to forget. Suddenly Louisa nodded her head gently in time to the music and he was arrested by the look of real enjoyment on her face. Without realizing what he was doing, he stepped forward to see what was amusing her so.

Louisa's position commanded a view of the ball-room and its crowded dancers. The tune was a lively country dance and the young couples were flinging themselves into it with the delighted abandon of small children playing a favorite game. Somehow the striving and jealousy and artificial pretensions had dropped away and the dancers were able to immerse themselves in the gaiety of the steps. They made a kaleidoscope of breathtaking color as they moved through their patterns on the floor, and Geffrey found himself seeing it all as though for the first time. He took a step closer and without intending to brushed against Louisa's skirts.

"Isn't it lovely?" she asked gaily, flashing him a quick smile before she looked back at the dancers. "They suddenly all seem to be so happy."

"The music perhaps," Lord Geffrey murmured awkwardly.

"Yes, it does make it very gay. But everyone seems to be enjoying the dance far more than usual," she added.

Geffrey looked at her curiously. She seemed to be as pleased as she supposed the dancers to be, despite the fact that she herself was without a partner.

22

"You are enjoying your Season, then?" he asked curiously.

"Oh, yes, far more than I expected to," she answered earnestly. She noticed the mocking look on his face and continued. "It seemed rather pointless when Papa first insisted on it. I will be living nearly all the time in the country, most likely," she ended wistfully.

Noticing her tone, Lord Geffrey frowned a moment, then asked, "Surely that gives you all the more reason to have a gay time to remember."

"Oh, it is not that I don't like the country, sir!" Louisa protested with a laugh. "I just always thought that this sort of thing wasn't for me. Young ladies like Melinda are the ones to have this sort of good time, for they have the pretty looks that the gentlemen admire."

"Then you are certainly among them, Miss Bardoff," he answered promptly.

Louisa laughed again. "How gallant you are to say that! I wasn't expecting you to, truly. I am far too plump, and too short, and my gowns—" Here she paused to find the right expression. "I suppose you could say that they are most conventional!" she ended with a gay laugh.

Lord Geffrey was a trifle nonplussed by such frankness. It was not in his experience to have a compliment met with rebuttal, but he rallied. "You have the loveliest eyes of the Season, Miss Bardoff, and they are the windows of the soul. At least that is what the poets say!" he retorted.

"What fustian! It does little good to be beautiful inside when one is enjoying a London Season!" she exclaimed. "Although I am sure that it is very nice on other occasions," she added candidly after a moment's thought. Lord Geffery could only laugh.

"Oh, dear!" she said unexpectedly.

Her attention had been attracted to an interesting tableau across the room, her mother being a central figure in the scene. Two ladies of matronly age and respectable appearance had suddenly encountered one another face to face in a doorway. There seemed to be some confusion as to who would step aside for the other. Postures erect, the feathers in their headdresses quivering, they glared at each other in haughty silence. In fact, to a knowledgeable eye, such as Lord Geffrey's, they appeared for all the world to be like two pugilists in the fighting ring, prepared to battle to the bitter end, so pugnacious was their mien.

Louisa suddenly stooped down and to Lord Geffrey's utter amazement, ripped a flounce from her skirt until it was dangling nearly to the floor.

"There, that should do quite nicely. If you will excuse me, my lord, I must leave you to enjoy this lovely view of the dancing in solitude," and casting another smile in his direction, she hurried to the contested doorway.

With growing amusement, Geffrey watched her

approach her mother with the torn flounce of her dress. The need for repairing such a frightful rent in her daughter's attire had far greater importance to Lady Bardoff than the challenge thrown in her face by her arch rival, Lady Howorthy. Pausing for only one contemptuous glance at the other matron, she hurried off after her daughter to one of the small sitting rooms set aside for just such a catastrophe, a room that was fortunately in the opposite direction of the contested doorway.

For a moment Lord Geffrey wondered how Louisa would have managed to get her mother past Lady Howorthy if their way had led them to the door. With a grin, he decided that she would probably have managed that as well. He turned toward the dance floor with more enthusiasm than he usually felt for these affairs and prepared to enjoy his evening, having forgotten his intention of discovering to what extent he owed Louisa's discretion for the general ignorance surrounding that embarrassing scene in the conservatory.

In another corner of the ballroom two dignified gentlemen of advanced middle age had observed the small scene and appreciated Louisa's *contretemps*. One of them had been more anxious than the other, uneasy about the embarrassing outcome of such a situation if his daughter had not intervened. Once the two ladies were skillfully separated, he breathed a sigh of relief and drank a hasty gulp of champagne.

The Earl of Whitworth smiled at his old friend fondly. "She is a clever girl, your Louisa. Far more so than my Melinda, I fear."

"I can't say but aye to the first of your sentiments, Whitworth, although you wrong your daughter. Melinda is a pretty little thing, they say a diamond of the first water. She is something you can be proud of."

"Pretty, but not clever."

"Maybe she hasn't had to be. Lord knows, Louisa's had more than her share of opportunity to practice common sense," her father said gloomily, delicately alluding to his beloved spouse's sometimes foolish behavior. The feud with Lady Howorthy had been going on for years, no one knew quite how long, which was an awkward state of affairs, in view of the close proximity of Howorthy Hill and Bardoff Hall. It was most inconvenient to have the two principal families of a neighborhood not on speaking terms.

Sir Harry's thoughts veered in another direction. "But there is something wrong with that rig she's in. Don't set her off to advantage. Don't know why. After all, her mother chose it and that *is* one thing that she ought to know about."

The Earl, more conversant with ladies' fashions than his friend, refrained from commenting on that observation. He was aware that Louisa's dress was in the mode generally expected of young ladies of her age, but without the imaginative alterations and touches that would have made it a more becoming gown. "Tommy Colville is a very lucky young man to have a young lady such as she," Whitworth said soothingly.

Instead of pleasing Sir Harry, he had unwittingly uncovered yet another grievance.

"That he is. But he had better appreciate what he is getting a bit more. That young pup don't have the sense of a peahen."

He brooded over his champagne glass, then gulped down the last of it.

The earl chuckled. "He's young yet, and army mad. Give him time. He'll learn."

"Why his father doesn't buy him a cornetcy I don't know. If he isn't careful, that lad will run off and enlist," Sir Harry complained with a grumble.

Whitworth was somber for a moment, toying thoughtfully with the fine silk of his cuffs. "I rather think that he hasn't come to appreciate young Tom's ardor in the matter. Lady Colville is dead set against it, I have heard."

Sir Harry agreed. "And she is probably throwing up a smoke screen in the matter, confusing the whole situation while she tries to keep her boy at her side and out of danger."

"She means well," Whitworth said deprecatingly.

"They all do, Whitty. They all do. That's just the problem. But he must grow up sometime."

And having found a sentiment that both could share, they went off in search of more champagne.

III

Tommy Colville was proudly displaying the fine points of his matched team of bays as he drove his high-perched phaeton through the park.

"See what sweet goers they are, Louisa? Look at the way they step," he said enthusiastically.

"They are a pretty color, Tommy," Louisa agreed cheerfully. Although she knew little of horses, and her seat was alarmingly high from the ground, she was enjoying the drive immensely. She judged that they must be traveling at a rate of nearly five miles an hour, an exhilarating experience in an open carriage. The sun shone brightly, the air was crisp, and she felt quite confident that the hat she was wearing, one of the few that she owned that had been her own choice entirely, was quite becoming to her, which it was. There were friends to wave to and occasionally she was able to persuade Tommy to pull up for a chat with some particularly dear intimate.

Tommy was looking at her with compassion. "It ain't so much the color that counts, Lou," he explained kindly.

"Then why don't you have horses with spots? Or perhaps one each of different colors? A brown one and a black one, perhaps?" she asked innocently.

"Well dash it, Lou, that wouldn't be the thing. Not at all!" Tommy protested.

"But you said that the colors don't matter," Louisa said indignantly. "Either they do or they don't, Tommy Colville."

Young Colville sputtered helplessly, then pulled up his team. This was going to take all of his powers of explanation to unravel and he needed to give it his undivided attention.

"You see, Louisa, the color of the horse doesn't change the way it goes. It's the shoulders and back and legs and hocks and things like that that make a difference. It's the way the animal moves that's important, and the spirit it has."

"And splints, Tommy? Do they help?"

Tommy groaned under his breath. "No, Lou, splints don't help," he explained.

"Oh. One hears so much about them, being thrown and all. I thought that they were important."

"They *are* important, damn it, Lou. They're something that goes wrong with a horse."

"You shouldn't use such language in my presence, Tommy. Only think, our mamas would not approve," Louisa protested solemnly.

Tommy winced, then apologized manfully. "Sorry, Louisa, it just slipped out. Nothing intended by it, no disrespect. I just keep forgetting that you're a girl, er, I mean a young lady . . ." He trailed off even more incoherently.

"That's quite all right, Tommy," Louisa answered with mock hauteur that hid a gleam in her eyes. "But you have yet to explain why the color of the animal is unimportant to the way the animal moves, but why matching two horses of the same color is important." She waited with all of her dignity for the much sought explanation.

"It is the rarity of such a matching of color and ability that makes it valuable, Miss Bardoff," a third voice interposed.

The young couple swung around in surprise, to discover that Lord Geffrey had come up behind them mounted on a fine stallion that immediately earned Tommy's awed admiration.

"Lord Geffrey," Louisa said with a smile, holding out her hand to him. "You know my cousin Tommy Colville, don't you?"

"I believe that I have seen Mr. Colville at Tattersall's on occasion," Lord Geffrey said with a smile as he bowed to the young man. "A fine pair of bays you have there, Colville. They were Quin's, weren't they? I heard that he had sold them."

Tommy could barely speak through the confusion the compliment had caused him. To have a renowned horseman such as Lord Geffrey compliment his team, his very own cattle, was an honor that he had not even dreamed of. "Thank you, sir. Yes, I got them off of Mr. Quin."

"Good choice," Lord Geffrey said with approval as he cast an expert eye over their legs.

Tommy blushed pink with pleasure. "My father did give me a word or two of advice, sir," he allowed honestly, then lapsed into silence. His admission earned him Geffrey's amused approval.

Louisa flung herself into the conversation. "Tommy was just telling me why they are a good choice. I don't see why the color is unimportant and then suddenly becomes very important. It is all very confusing to me."

Lord Geffrey smiled at her with amusement. "Perhaps I can draw an analogy for you, Miss Bardoff," he offered helpfully.

"Please do," she answered promptly, settling back as comfortably as she dared in her high seat and waiting expectantly for some further amusement.

"It is a question of the usefulness of an object being of primary importance and appearance of secondary value. For example, your hat protects your eyes from the brightness of the sunshine, your head from the dampness of the rain. That is its primary importance and purpose."

Louisa's hands flew up to the confection of straw and flowers that perched on top of her head. Any protection that it provided was slight indeed.

"But it has still another value. It is a very charming hat, one that draws attention to the beauty of its wearer. And so its appearance, its color and matching so to speak, while not of practical importance, does have value."

Louisa giggled, both at Lord Geffrey's nonsense and at Tommy's confusion.

"I think that you are teasing me, sir. You have it turned around, surely!" she retorted.

"Turned around?" Lord Geffrey asked in surprise. Then with a look of exaggerated comprehension, he said, "But of course. Forgive me. It is the wearer who gives charm to the hat. Thank you for correcting my error, Miss Bardoff. You are entirely in the right!"

Louisa laughed. "No, no. Lord Geffrey. You are *too* bad, really you are. My hat is of no practical use whatsoever, and you know it. The brim does nothing to shade my face from the sun and the whole thing would dissolve if a single drop of rain should touch it."

"But I still maintain that it serves a practical purpose, Miss Bardoff. If it adds yet one more charming detail to the already lovely picture the wearer presents, it has been useful indeed. Don't you concur with me, Colville?"

Louisa was helpless with laughter and Tommy seized the opportunity to bring the conversation back to its original topic. "Well, mere show don't work for horses," he said practically. "It's all very well and good to talk about pretty gewgaws being useful and important, I enjoy them myself," he explained earnestly. "But a horse has its job to do, too, you know."

"Quite right, Colville," Lord Geffrey agreed with a grin. "Take those grays over there," he continued, nodding at a team across the road.

"Them!" Tommy snorted with disgust. "Clumsy, awkward team they are."

As the two men began to discuss the relative merits of the teams and drivers on display in the park, Louisa listened with far more interest than she had felt before. Lord Geffrey's comments showed him to be knowledgeable, even expert, but his descriptions and explanations were amusing and surprisingly easy for her to understand. Had she but know it, she would have been flattered by the effort that he was making to make the conversation one that would amuse her.

Lord Geffrey was watching the two young people with interest. Colville was a nice enough boy, easy to like despite his youth and inexperience. Geffrey thought that the youngster was army mad, his suspicions founded on occasional references to military figures and their mounts. He also thought that the young couple were far from being in love with one another. They were perfectly at ease in each other's company, in the manner of childhood friends who had played together and had much in common. He suspected that as long as this status quo was maintained, their proposed marriage had every chance of success. Louisa's good sense and Tommy's amiability would go far toward building their affection into a sound and happy marriage.

Their chatter was interrupted by yet more arrivals. Lady Colville, Tommy's mother, hailed them from the comfortable seats of her landau, which she shared with Susan Lauderdale, a connection of the Bardoffs who, with her mother, lived in that family's household. Louisa's best friend, she was a pretty girl with a sweet disposition and generally well liked, although her lack of a portion hampered her chances of making a good match.

"Tommy, dear, do hand Louisa down from that dreadfully high seat! It is wrong of you to expose her to such danger! What will people think?" Lady Colville protested faintly.

"Dash it, Mama, she is perfectly safe. You've come to no harm, have you, Lou?"

"None at all, Lady Colville. I did rather fear at one point that the excessive height would make me dizzy and would cause me to fall, but that has not been the case," she assured the lady cheerfully.

Lady Colville screamed. "Tommy! Louisa! How foolish you both are. Why your father ever let you get that phaeton and those horses I don't know, Tommy. Lord Geffrey, do, do come to an anxious mother's aid and hand Louisa out of that dreadful seat! If anything befalls her and it is laid at my Tommy's door, I shall never be able to face her mother, never!"

Somewhat sulkily, Tommy had already climbed down to the ground and was helping Louisa down. This young lady grinned sympathetically, then climbed up into the landau to a seat next to Lady Colville.

"I think that it is a lovely team, Lady Colville," she said cheerfully. "So beautifully matched. And Tommy is an excellent driver, I can assure you."

"They are still an awful danger to Tommy!" Lady Colville said with doom in her voice. "Why gentlemen must be interested in such things I can't understand!" Poor Tommy was squirming with embarrassment as the apron strings so firmly maintained by his mother were thus so ruthlessly exposed.

Lord Geffrey smiled reassuringly at the youngster, then skillfully directed the conversation to safer topics. The party was quietly augmented by one more member, John Howorthy, a boon companion of Tommy's, who appeared on his own mount and was greeted by the subdued heir of the Colvilles with relief. Lady Colville waved casually to him, this being all the attention that she could spare as she continued to describe with horror the bonnet she had seen in the park the day before. John sidled his horse over to Susan Lauderdale's side of the carriage and a very quiet conversation ensued between those two under the cover of the more animated talk of the others.

Geffrey watched the group with considerable curiosity. John was the son of Lady Howorthy of the doorway confrontation and should have been unpopular among the rest of the Bardoff clan if the animosity between the matrons was indicative of a family feud. His friendship with Tommy Colville explained his acceptance by the group to some extent, but Geffrey guessed that the attitude of the others was also influenced by their lack of support or even understanding of the ladies' bitter quarrel. His attentions to Miss Lauderdale were curious. The young lady's blushes told him that they were welcomed and perhaps already familiar to her. Louisa's anxious and affectionate glances in their direction confirmed his suspicions. An affection seemed to exist between the son of the dreadful Lady Howorthy and a young lady who relied on the kindness of the redoubtable Lady Bardoff for her home and her Season. Lord Geffrey suspected that even Louisa's ability to deal with her mother would be strained if this relationship was allowed to develop into a more particular partiality.

Lady Colville seemed unaware of the interesting

conversation taking place next to her. Her indifference was well known, fashion being her only interest outside her family and that a feeble one. Her ability to recognize that a courtship was taking place under her nose was nil, especially when she had no personal interest in the principals.

There arose a general agreement to retire to the Colville's town house for refreshments, encouraged by Lady Colville's faint complaints about the exhaustion induced by riding about in her well sprung landau and the strain of greeting so many friends. They were soon ambling toward the park's entrance, Lord Geffrey accompanying them on the laughing insistence of Louisa and Tommy. The party made its way to Park Street, where Lady Colville promptly retired to her boudoir for a much needed rest.

This made little difference in the disposition of the party. To Lord Geffrey's surprise, Louisa was accepted as hostess by all concerned, including the elderly butler. The dignified Ross unbent so far as to smile at Miss Louisa, hurry his minions off to do her bidding, and murmur something confidentially into her ear about the distress of the very expensive French chef.

"Do excuse me for a moment, everyone. There is one little thing that I must see to," she said as she flitted out of the room. Lord Geffrey found himself thrown back into a discussion of horses with Tommy Colville while Miss Lauderdale and John

Howorthy retired to a window overlooking a diminutive garden where they talked very quietly.

When Louisa returned Tommy broke off his description of a sorrel mare. "I say, Lou, shall I go to my club for dinner tonight or will André be in a good humor?"

"His name is Etienne, Tommy, and if someone else would just take the time to speak a little French to him, or even to get his name right, you would feast handsomely every night of the week at your mother's table. He cannot make head or tail of what anyone on the staff is saying, and he finds that very upsetting."

"Well, they can't figure him out, either, Lou," Tommy answered reasonably.

"But Tommy, they can 'figure out' one another. He has no one to talk to and he is lonely," she protested.

Seeing that the conversation was settling into well worn grooves, Lord Geffrey rose to make his departure. It was all very well to associate with mere striplings and school room misses, but when the children started to squabble it was time for men of experience and judgement to leave.

"My thanks for your hospitality, Colville," he said somewhat formally.

Tommy, brought back to his responsibilities as a host, returned his guest's bow with solemn dignity, suddenly striving to be a man of the world.

"Good of you to find time for us, sir. I enjoyed our conversation exceedingly. Most illuminating."

Amused, Geffrey relented. "Perhaps you would enjoy a trip to Tattersall's with me sometime, Colville." Seeing the eager pleasure on the young man's face, and receiving a grateful smile from Louisa, he was encouraged to go on. "Next Thursday, perhaps? And Mr. Howorthy is to accompany us, of course, if he desires."

"Oh, sir, that would be smashing! Just the thing! It is good of you to invite us, sir!"

And on a note of benign generosity, Lord Geffrey left the young couples to their own amusements and rode to his own establishment to prepare for the evening's social engagements.

IV

─────────◆─────────

What Lord Geffrey left behind him was a council of war.

"I say, Louisa. Do you have any idea of why the Mater and your mother are at dagger points?" John Howorthy asked tentatively. "It's dashed inconvenient."

"Inconvenient! It is worse than that! They nearly created a scene last night at the Saltire ball."

"Good thing your flounce tore, Lou. Lucky," Tommy commented thoughtfully.

"Lucky?" Louisa said with awful intensity. "Lucky?"

The young man looked at her in surprise, while Susan smiled. "I think that Louisa made her own luck last night," the young lady explained to her friend.

"What do you mean by that?" John asked.

"She tore the flounce herself, I rather imagine," Susan answered promptly.

Tommy looked at Louisa with awe. "I say, Lou, that was *very* good thinking. I never would have come up with that myself," he said with simple admiration.

"I don't see how you *could* have thought of it, Tommy. You haven't any flounces!" She then relented and smiled at him to take the sting from her retort.

"Well, you have far too many if you ask me," he answered, determined to have the last word in the exchange.

Louisa looked down thoughtfully at the rows and rows of ruffles along the bottom edge of her skirt. They made her short, plump figure appear even fuller, almost to the point of being squat. "I am afraid that you are right, Tommy," she agreed sadly. "But Mama says that it's the thing."

Susan hastily intervened. "But what of the quarrel? Does anybody know anything about how it started?"

"My mother says that Louisa's mother snubbed her right from the beginning, just as soon as she and Father were married," John said apologetically.

"That seems strange. Your grandmother was her godmother, you know. I mean that the Dowager

Lady Howorthy was Mama's godmother," Louisa explained. "They were very fond of one another, judging from what Mama says about her. Her proudest possessions are two wall hangings in the great hall in the country house. Dowager Lady Howorthy did most of the needlework and Mama helped her considerably. She is quite sentimental about them."

"Can't think why," Tommy said judiciously. "They are both damned dismal, if you ask me."

Susan giggled. "You don't find the scenes from the life of Cleopatra edifying?" she teased. "Sending Antony Off to Fight Octavius, and Entering Rome with Julius Ceasar?"

"Is that what they are?" Tommy asked with surprise. "Couldn't tell, what with the way they are rigged out. Why'd your grandmother do a thing like that?"

John shrugged good naturedly. "She went through an Egyptian period, I suppose. We have another wall hanging like that in our country house. There is even a room full of Indian artifacts from South America, and another of Turkish rugs and waterpipes. She would develop an enthusiasm for something and throw herself into it, at least that is how my father explains it. I never knew her myself, so I can't say. She died just before my parents were married."

"Perhaps that is it," Louisa cried out with excitement. "Mama could have felt that they married too soon after the Dowager's death! That wouldn't have been showing a proper regard for her, and Mama would have disliked that immensely."

John looked doubtful about this. "Aunt Enderbie wasn't offended, and she is a high stickler for that sort of thing. Far more so than your mother is ever likely to be, Lou."

"Then what could it be?" Susan asked, her dismay eloquent in her tone and expression. For the first time Louisa was sure of what she had long suspected: that her dearest friend Susan was truly in love with John Howorthy.

In many ways it would make a good match. Susan was of respectable family of good lineage, a matter of importance to John's mother, who was from only an obscure county family and placed great value on such things. Her own considerable wealth had enabled the Howorthy family to renew its position of prominence in their part of the world, and so Lady Howorthy could afford to place great stock in family connections.

Susan was distantly related to several great families, but always through a long line of younger sons of impoverished younger sons. Without the generosity of her schoolfriend Marie Bardoff, Mrs. Lauderdale would have been hard-pressed to maintain herself and her daughter in a respectable way, far less to arrange for her presentation this Season. Lady Bardoff was generously providing the wherewithal for Susan's gowns, insisting good naturedly that it was a minor matter, especially in view of the fact that she must already go to the trouble of equipping and presenting her own daughter. Susan was dressed, as was Louisa, to Lady Bardoff's taste and had been included in all of the plans and activities for the Season.

It was this very generosity that had brought about their present dilemma. Lady Bardoff, who had been a most generous and good natured benefactress, adamantly refused to have a Howorthy, any Howorthy, in her home. She turned a blind eye to Tommy's friendship with John, comforting herself quite rightly that it was none of her business and boys will be boys. Besides, there was nothing that she could do about it. To raise a protest would offend Lord and Lady Colville, who accepted John with tolerance for their son's sake and had even grown to be quite fond of him. But if Lady Bardoff had been aware of the degree of intimacy that had arisen between Susan and John, she would have been horrified, and Mrs. Lauderdale, who supported her in all things, would have rushed forward to put an end to the budding romance, whatever her daughter's feelings in the matter.

The four young people looked at one another glumly, each aware of the tangle of the situation.

"It would appear to me that we must do something to end this feud," Louisa said suddenly, a note of decision in her voice.

John refused to be heartened by her show of confidence. "How are we going to do that? This feud apparently began before any of us were born," he said glumly.

Louisa refused to be turned aside from her purpose. "We might find out what started it and then try to set it aright."

The others looked at her doubtfully. "How are we to do that, Lou?" Tommy finally asked.

"We shall try to find out from the people who ought to know, who were alive then and friendly with both families. For example, your Aunt Enderbie, John."

John suddenly brightened. "That's the very thing, Lou! Aunt Enderbie might even be able to give us advice. She don't approve of this sort of quarrel. Bad *Ton*."

"And your grandmother, Tommy, the Dowager Lady Colville. She would know *something*."

Tommy was less enthusiastic than was his friend John. "But how can I do that, Lou? I can't just walk up to her and ask her about it point-blank, can I? She's bound to want to know what it is all about that I am suddenly interested in another family's business."

Everyone's hopes were momentarily dashed. "Well, can't you get it out of her indirectly? Ask her about the past? Or say that you want to know more about what it was like when your parents were young and just married?" Louisa pressed.

Tommy snorted. "Ain't my style, Lou. She will smell something fishy in a minute."

"Oh," Louisa said, disheartened. In all truth, she had not been impressed with her own argument either. There were several moments of hard—thinking silence.

"But wait," Susan said unexpectedly. "Why can't we do just that? Why can't we just ask people outright?"

"Sounds dashed impertinent, that's why," Tommy grumbled.

"No, no. Let her finish," John said, looking at her adoringly.

"You and Louisa are supposed to get married, aren't you? I mean, it is not official, but everyone has taken it for granted ever since I can remember."

"No announcement yet," Tommy said, "but that's what our parents have planned."

"Well, which of your friends will stand up with you in the ceremony?" she asked.

"John, of course."

"And if John is invited, who else should receive an invitation?"

"My parents," John said, comprehension dawning.

"It would be most unusual if they weren't invited," Susan added.

"Scandalous!" Louisa agreed cheerfully.

"And so if the feud isn't settled, there will be a

frightful amount of difficulty over the wedding. Lady Howorthy ought to be present, but Lady Bardoff won't admit her to her home," Susan expounded.

"And the sensible thing for us to do is to settle this silly quarrel before the wedding takes place," Louisa finished, flourishing her arms with excitement.

"Exactly," Susan agreed.

John looked at his beloved with newfound respect. "The very thing!"

"Simple, direct, and totally unexceptional," Louisa said happily.

"Unless they find out about Susan and John before then," Tommy muttered under his breath apprehensively. Louisa shushed him but the others had not heard his comment, in any case. They were sitting in the window seat, holding hands and gazing lovingly into one another's eyes.

"Then we have a great deal of work to do," Louisa announced with determination. "We must set about this at once. First we shall make a list of likely people to ask, then decide which of us shall talk to them. Agreed?"

"Agreed," John said enthusiastically.

"Just one thing," Tommy said stubbornly.

"Yes?" Louisa asked apprehensively.

He glanced at his best friend and Susan, awkwardly playing with his suddenly too tight neckcloth. An embarrassed flush rose in his face, but he persevered.

"There will be a horrible row if your mama and Lady Bardoff hear that you and Susan have, well, uh . . . You know, John," he finished hurriedly.

There was an embarrassed silence. Thus far the clandestine nature of the courtship had gone unremarked in the group, everyone implicitly accepting the honorable intentions of the lovers as opposed to the cruel necessity of silence. Only Lady Colville had possibly been in a position to raise objections, but she was as indifferent to the ramifications of the friendship as she was to everything else.

"Then we will have to stop seeing one another. Not even to talk together at balls and parties," Susan said with sudden decision that surprised her friends.

Tommy heaved a sigh of relief. "Dashed good of you to understand, Sue. Awkward."

"But I can't not ever talk to her! It may take months and months to sort this out," John protested heatedly.

"We must, dearest," Susan pleaded. "If Mama discovers that we have been seeing one another and that our regard is such as it is, if she discovers this before the feud is settled, we will never have a chance of getting married." She suddenly blushed at her own forthrightness, but the others were relieved that it had finally been said openly.

"You can send messages, and notes, too, if we

are very careful about it," Louisa said encouragingly.

"You can give the note to me and then I will give it to Louisa and then Louisa will give it to Susan!" Tommy said triumphantly.

Louisa giggled. "Everyone will think that Tommy and I are exchanging love notes."

"Bosh!" Tommy said explosively. "As if we two would bother with such nonsense."

"It would be very romantic," Louisa protested wistfully.

"No point in it, Lou. Our parents allow us to talk to each other."

Louisa thought that that was no reason against the practice, but forbore to comment further to her forthright fiance.

"And now we can start the list," Susan said briskly, interrupting the badinage.

"Fetch pen and paper, Tommy. We've work to do!" Louisa ordered him briskly.

"This had better succeed," John said grimly. "If it fails, I will have to take a hint from Grandmother's Cleopatra tapestry and carry Susan off wrapped in a carpet."

"John!" his friend protested manfully. "Damned silly thing for you to do!"

Susan blushed furiously. "Oh, John!"

And they set to work.

V

Their first efforts to unravel the mystery were highly unsatisfactory. John had naturally been assigned his Aunt Enderbie and in view of that lady's presence in London, he was encouraged to seek an interview immediately. As Louisa pointed out, the solution to their problem could easily be within their grasp. Tommy added that he wasn't going to tackle his grandmother, and travel way out into the country to do so, unless it was absolutely necessary.

John approached his redoubtable relative's home with some trepidation. Although he had been thoroughly rehearsed in his role by Susan and Louisa, his boyhood fear of Aunt Enderbie was in the forefront of his mind.

Charlotte Henrietta Howorthy Enderbie was a lady of the previous century. In her youth she had flung herself with gusto into the pleasures of life in those more permissive days, taking interest in everything from Walpole's little Gothic castle at Strawberry Hill, to traveling the rough roads of the period on innumerable visits to relatives and friends. She had followed the hunt, dabbled in medical research when she submitted to a smallpox vaccination, been enthralled by *Pamela*, celebrated Wolfe's victory on the Heights of Abraham, and disdained Lord Dacre's alterations of his home Belhaus. Her costume still reflected the end of that era, with her long-waisted dresses (now returning to style, much to her glee), panniers and monstrous large calashes to cover an elaborate hair structure on the few occasions she left her home. Now in her late eighties, her many escapades were but awed tales cherished in whispers by a large tribe of nieces and nephews. Her late husband, Mr. Enderbie, a man of acceptable family, tolerable person, and enormous fortune, had left his entire estate to his widow, their only child having died in infancy. She now capitalized on her old age and great wealth to express her disdain for the present century in sharp criticisms and a seemingly capricious insistance on the finer points of etiquette. Those of whom she approved were treated with charm and tolerance, others were bullied. It had long since been apparent to John that his mother fell into the latter category. Of his own standing he was uncertain.

A middle-aged butler, grandson of Aunt Enderbie's first retainer from the days when she had been newly married, showed John into the small drawing room with suitable dignity, clearly stating by his mien that the visitor was no longer the little boy who had begged for just one more sweet. With a bow, he left John to face his aunt.

"Stand in the light, young man! How can you expect me to see you if you linger in the shadows? Come here by the window and let me have a look at you."

With this unhappy opening depressing his spirits, John approached the small bay window where his aunt sat. From her comfortable armchair she could enjoy the warmth of the sunlight flooding in through the windows and admire what her gardeners had done with a small patch of ground beneath her view. John walked toward her with caution, almost tiptoeing, carefully watching every word and gesture he made to be sure that he forgot no small point of polite usage in dealing with his aunt.

When he was seated in his chair, a most uncomfortable one with a hard seat and a straight back, and a light refreshment had been placed on the small round table between them, his aunt fell silent. She clearly expected him to state his business. Her look of expectancy filled him with dread and he cast about in his mind for some acceptable conversational gambit.

"Nice weather we have been having, Aunt," he said brightly.

She looked out the window and inspected the skies. "The sun does seem to be shining."

"Pretty garden there." He nodded toward the wintery scene beyond the window.

She glanced at the dismal picture with surprise. "Quite."

"Nice to have the sun shining on it."

"Oh?"

John blundered to a halt, realizing that a change of tactics was necessary to recover the ground he had lost with his aimless chatter.

"Aunt, I am here for a friend of mine, Tommy Colville," he explained.

"Why can't Thomas come himself?"

"Well, you see, it is a rather complicated situation, and because I am related to you we thought that I ought to ask you."

"We?"

"Tommy and Lou . . . I mean Tommy and I thought that I should ask you."

Aunt Enderbie looked at him carefully, secretly amused by his predicament, curiosity growing.

" 'Ask'? What would you ask of me? Are you in debt? From gambling, perhaps?"

"Dash it all, Aunt, nothing like *that*! Even if we

were at *point non plus* we wouldn't approach you. Not the thing!"

"Then are the two of you planning on some new business venture that requires capital?"

"Tommy and I wouldn't know how to enter into business!" he protested indignantly, more stung by this accusation than the other one. "We certainly wouldn't ask you for money. Besides, we don't need to. Both pretty plump in the pocket."

"I am so glad to hear that," she said. Once again the silence grew.

John was startled to find that the conversational initiative once more rested with him. He tried to organise his thoughts, but Aunt Enderbie, judging from his expression, knew that he was not having much luck at it.

"You were going to ask me something?" she said kindly.

"Oh, yes, I suppose that I was," John managed to say.

"For your friend Tommy?"

"That's it! Now I have it straight! You see, Tommy is going to marry Louisa Bardoff, a family arrangement."

"And you feel he needs some assistance?" Aunt Enderbie asked in mock alarm. Wicked thoughts of John assisting Tommy Colville came to mind. There was a particularly amusing vision of a honeymoon trip for three . . . ? This conversation was proving to be even more amusing than she had heretofore expected.

"Well, you know, Aunt. It's the thing to do. Stand by him during the ceremony, cheer him up the night before, make sure that he doesn't lose the ring," he explained earnestly.

"Ah! And is my assistance needed also? I could perhaps hold the ring for him until the time that it is needed. I apprehend that the activities of the evening before the ceremony might make that a wise precaution."

"Oh, no, ma'am, not at all. Not that."

"Then what?"

John decided that he had best finish his argument quickly. Any more interruptions might make it impossible to continue.

"If I play such a role in the ceremony, my parents ought to be present. They are acquainted with the Colvilles, in any case, and it would be scandalous if they don't get an invitation."

"Scandalous? Not necessarily," Aunt Enderbie considered the point judiciously. "If only a small company is invited it would not seem unusual to limit the guest list."

"Louisa wants a big wedding."

"Ah. Then so it should be. Have them invited, by all means. Your mama will hardly be noticeable in a really large crowd."

"But that is the problem," John said desperately, ignoring the jibe directed against his parent.

"Oh?"

"Lady Bardoff and the Mater ain't on speaking terms. Been like that for years. Lady Bardoff won't have her in her home, snubs her at the few parties they both attend."

"I never knew that Lady Bardoff had such sense! And your mother bears this with Christian fortitude, I imagine?" Aunt Enderbie asked maliciously.

"Oh, no. She gives as good as she gets."

"I rather thought that that would be the case."

"And so, you see, if the bride's family, especially the mother, issues the invitations, my mother won't get one. There would be a scandal!" he finished triumphantly.

"Then I suggest that you withdraw from such a prominent role in the ceremony," his aunt advised calmly.

John stared at her with his mouth wide open. "But, but, but. . . . Tommy's my best friend!" He looked at her with dismay, then added, suddenly inspired, "He insists!"

Aunt Enderbie was beginning to suspect that there was something more afoot than she had been told, or would be told. Once again, she resorted to silence. John seized his opportunity.

"And so we want to settle the quarrel and we thought that if we knew what had started it, we could go from there."

"Very laudable! A peace mission," she said thoughtfully. "And my role?"

"We thought that you would know! Know what they are both so upset about."

"My dear John, if I knew *that* I would have ended this nonsense long ago. It is all such bad *Ton!*"

John was crestfallen. He sat gazing at her helplessly, his hopes for an easy solution dashed.

Aunt Enderbie looked at him thoughtfully, her mind probing the likely reasons for this outrageous plan of his. There must be something, some other explanation for his sudden desire to end the feud that dated back to before his birth. Reconciliation with the Bardoff family would be the main reward of his efforts, and she thought that she saw a glimmer of his true motives.

"It began soon after your parents were married. Lady Bardoff was quite cordial, initially. She had been fond of her godmother, the Dowager Lady Howorthy and was a near neighbor, so her kindness was to be expected. Then for no apparent reason a coldness sprang up between the two ladies. You were born that spring and your parents were little seen in Town. And then Louisa was born that autumn. I hear that she is a charming young lady."

"So it wasn't any impropriety in the wedding that upset Lady Bardoff," John mused to himself, ignoring the bait.

"Impropriety in the wedding? Surely *not!* Not in this family, at least as long as I am still alive," the elderly lady said indignantly.

"We thought that it followed pretty closely on the heels of Grandmother's death and that Louisa's mother might have disapproved of it on that count."

"Not at all. It was quite a small, private ceremony and Lady Bardoff was very friendly. In fact, she attended the ceremony. I fear that the answer to your mystery lies with Lady Bardoff. Somehow I think that your mother, whatever her faults may be, was confused by the change in that lady's attitude and merely responded with more unkindness. Perhaps you should ask your Louisa to sound out her mother."

"Lou?" John was suddenly covered with confusion, much to his aunt's satisfaction. "I suppose that she could do that. But then it might make matters worse. Her mother has never breathed a word to her about it."

"It is a tactic worth considering."

"Dashed hard for her."

"If her reasons are strong enough she will certainly undertake the task, don't you think?"

John blushed, wondering if Louisa's affection for his dearest Susan, was strong enough for such a sacrifice. To tackle Lady Bardoff could bring weeks of scolding and disgrace down on her head. He was unaware that his aunt was watching him narrowly, seeking to understand his embarrassment and drawing her own conclusions.

"Is there any great urgency in the matter?" she

asked him with more kindness than she had hitherto shown.

"Yes! There certainly is! The whole thing is one big, tangled mess!" John answered glumly.

"Then you will have to keep at it. The elder Lady Colville might know something about it. Before she was plagued with ill health, she was much about and knew of all the gossip."

"Thank you, Aunt. We had thought she might help, but with her retired to the country, it will necessitate Tommy doing a bit of traveling to reach her. We thought to start with you in the hope that you could solve the problem immediately."

"Tommy is certainly very eager in the matter," Aunt Enderbie observed dryly.

"Tommy's the greatest chap! Best friend a fellow ever had. He would do anything for me and I for him."

"Then I am sure that he will set out immediately for his grandmother's home. Prompt action seems called for."

"By jove, you're right!" John said eagerly. Then a thought occurred to him. "But not before Thursday. Lord Geffrey has invited him to attend the auction at Tattersall's with him, you see," he explained with simple pride.

"Young Francis Geffrey?" his aunt asked in surprise. "I would have thought that his years placed him outside your circle of friends."

"Actually, I think he likes Louisa. But he's a

great go, top of the tree, even if he is so old! You should see him handle the ribbons!" John said enthusiastically.

"He cannot be more than thirty, John. That is not so old, let me assure you," she scolded.

"Oh, no, of course not, ma'am! He just don't act toplofty with us. Tommy said he even had Louisa understanding something of horses, and *that's* an achievement."

"I am glad that a man of substance and experience has condescended to associate with you. You will do well to observe every detail of his manner and dress. You could learn much from him." Her censorious eye rested on the somewhat unusual hue of her nephew's new waistcoat.

"I remember his father quite well, John. He was a handsome man and one of considerable charm. The ladies all lost their hearts to him."

Forgetting his unfortunate waistcoat, John decided that business was over and settled as comfortably as he could into his chair. He was regaled for the rest of the hour with tales of romances and escapades from his aunt's youth. To his surprise, he found it most entertaining. She had known everyone who was anyone and was not the least bit squeamish about admitting to friendships with some of the wilder elements of Society. Elopements, duels, wild practical jokes, vast gambling losses, all were recounted with spicy wit and references to the great events and people of the day. The visit ended with a warm invitation to come again and an offer of help if there was any she could render in his project. To herself she promised that she would discover more about her nephew's delightfully tangled affairs, especially as they related to the person of Miss Louisa Bardoff.

John's friends were less pleased than he with the outcome of his visit.

"She couldn't tell you anything?" Louisa asked wistfully for the third time, thinking of the absent Susan.

"She told me quite a lot, actually, all about what our parents were like back then and even our grandparents and some of . . ."

"But what about the quarrel? You said that she knew nothing of it!" she protested.

"No, she didn't. Said she would have settled it herself if she had known what it was all about. I can't believe it, but she must have been quite the thing in her day . . ."

"Dash it, John! That's of no import. You've achieved exactly nothing," Tommy said severely.

John defended himself vigorously. "That's not the case at all! She offered to help in any way she could . . ."

"Which is not at all," Tommy pointed out scathingly.

"And she offered a suggestion about whom to ask!"

Louisa's eyes lit up. "So there is someone who she thinks knows all about it."

"Exactly!" John said with satisfaction.

"But who, John? Who?" his friends asked eagerly.

John looked at them a trifle smugly. "Why, Lady Bardoff, of course. Aunt Enderbie says she don't think the Mater knows a thing, that it all started with Lady Bardoff taking offense at something. Sorry, Lou, no disrespect intended, but . . ."

"John, that is absolutely no use at all! None whatsoever!" Tommy exploded.

"We already know that Mama knows what it is all about," Louisa added impatiently.

"So why don't you ask her?" John asked with great simplicity.

"Because, because . . ."

"Lou, all you have to do is go up to her and ask her. Indirectly, of course. It is as simple as that," John said confidently.

Louisa thought for a moment. Her mother, usually the most amiable of ladies, was inclined to be stubborn on what she considered to be certain matters of great import. Once Lady Bardoff reached her decision it was irrevocable and beyond the remedy of reason. And these were the rare times when her usually voluble mama refused to discuss an event, especially with a mere child, even though the eldest. Not even Sir Harry was privy to the reasoning, or lack of it, that had led to her decision.

"She would not approve of my broaching the subject, truly she wouldn't. She would be greatly offended," Louisa said earnestly.

"I fear that Lou is right in the matter, John," Tommy added by way of support. "We might find the situation become irrevocable if Lady Bardoff feels that we are meddling."

"But what are we to do if no one else can tell us what is the matter?" John asked with dismay. "If Aunt Enderbie is right in her suspicions, not even my mother knows how it all began."

Gloom was settling over the three young people. Their task seemed to be impossible.

"We will just have to make sure of that," Louisa said, a trifle tearfully. "We cannot know that until we have asked everyone who might be able to help."

"I suppose that I must seek out the Dowager and talk with her," Tommy said with a sigh. "But I am not leaving until after Thursday," he added stubbornly.

"Yes, there is Almack's Assembly Wednesday evening," Louisa agreed, forgetful of Tommy's personal engagement in the excitement and importance of her own.

"While you are gone we shall seek out the other

people who could be of possible help," John added hopefully.

"And if all else fails," here Louisa paused for dramatic effect, "I will just have to speak with Mama."

VI

Almack's was Louisa's first trial by fire, or so she thought. Her previous social engagements had been in the congenial surroundings provided by family and friends, in the homes and company of people who wished her well.

The patronesses of Almack's Assembly Rooms had no reason at all to wish her well. They didn't even know her, a mere baronet's daughter without pretensions to either pretty looks or charm. True, Lady Cowper had been most charming about the vouchers and had even smiled at Louisa when she visited the Bardoff ladies to share a saucer of tea. But Lady Castlereagh was a notorious stickler and Princess Esterhazy . . . Well, she was a princess!

Lady Jersey was a notoriously malicious gossip and chatterbox and undoubtedly could not be bothered to show kindness to yet one more young debutante; that condescension was too much to expect. In fact, if she committed a faux pas, blundered unforgivably, forgot some minor point of etiquette, so much the better. She would provide grist for the gossip mills that were constantly grinding and in need of constant replenishment.

By the afternoon of the day, Louisa was sure that they were all anticipating her abject failure in their exclusive rooms. She began to positively detest the very thought of Almack's and rather wished that her mother would lose the vouchers and tickets. Perhaps a fire would break out? Or lightning strike! There possibilities did seem highly unlikely, unfortunately, but she continued to pray.

A declaration of war! The very thing. With Napoleon still on Elba so near the Continent, this was a much better possibility. But then, the thought of her brother Ruston enlisting intruded itself, squelching her desire for that event. If war broke out, Ruston would be off like a bolt of lightning, anxious to participate somehow or other.

There seemed to be no escape. Her gown had been laid out neatly on her bed by her abigail against the moment she was to don it. Louisa bitterly considered pouring ink on it. Without an appropriate gown, she could not be expected to attend this horror. And to her mind, the ink stains would be a positive improvement on the frilly pink dress. The very thing! Only the memory of closets *full* of such gowns held her back.

Louisa's thoughts continued rebelliously as the preparations for the evening proceeded. Her silence went unnoticed in the general bustle, everyone assuming that she was as happily excited as Susan, so obviously in anticipation of this major social event. Almack's admitted only the elite of Society, those who passed through its portals having met its patronesses' rigid standards of breeding and grace, or good amusement value. To attend was to be marked as a member of the *Haut Ton,* moving in the best circles of Society. What girl wouldn't be pleased at the prospect of an evening there?

Louisa suspected that the beauties of the Season enjoyed themselves immensely at Almack's. After all, it was known as the Marriage Mart, and an acknowledged beauty would have a string of suitors in attendance, with a busy evening ahead of her as she flirted and teased with them all. Susan, a very pretty girl, would have a pleasant enough time. Louisa had no illusions about her own success that night. Few of her brother's friends would be there to stand up good naturedly with their childhood playmate. Few relatives would be attending, the exception being her mama's mama, and that was not a pleasing thought, in view of that lady's acid tongue. Poor Tommy and Ruston were being positively forced to attend under the direst threats from their mothers, and they could be counted on to sulk throughout the evening. Even Papa was grumbling about spending an evening in the company of some he chose to label bounders and upstarts, his old fashioned standards offended by the looser ways of the modern world. That a large number of partners would flock to dance with plain, rather dowdy Miss Bardoff was doubtful.

But her hair was dressed in suitable curls, the gown slipped onto her plump figure, and they were all in the carriage, driving sedately to Almack's, beyond any hope of recall.

Their arrival was unexceptional. Fortunately for Louisa's peace of mind, Lady Cowper greeted them at the door. This amiable lady was kindness itself, talking to them in a friendly manner that proclaimed to all her approval of the two young ladies being presented. She pressed them to join the dancers, and soon an unwilling Tommy was leading Louisa into a country dance, followed closely by Ruston and Susan.

The dance was a gay one, the musicians excellent in their lively playing, and soon even Tommy was enjoying himself.

"Not bad so far, eh, Lou?" he said at the end of the dance. "Just like any other ball or party."

His tone of sophistication and worldliness, coupled with his sudden nonchalance, irritated the still nervous Louisa unbearably.

"That is all very well for you to say, Tommy

Colville! No one is counting the number of dances you sit out! You have done your duty by me and can now abandon me to a chair next to Mama for the rest of the evening." Her lower lip trembled with indignation.

Tommy looked at her with surprise. This was the first time she had ever worried about sitting out a dance. "Well, dash it all, Lou, I'll stand up with you once more! I'm to get Lady Cowper's permission for the waltz. That's the drill, ain't it?"

Louisa could only sigh with exasperation at this example of wanton unfeeling as they walked across the room.

"I thought you'd like that," he continued peevishly. "Can't say why you should, but everyone else says it's dashed important. And I can only stand up with you twice because your grandmother is here and she's such a stickler."

The reminder of that august lady's presence did little for Louisa's peace of mind. "Perhaps Ruston will dance with me!" she said desperately. "If not, I shall have to spend the whole of the evening with Grandmother!"

Tommy suddenly appreciated her dilemma. "I could ask my friends to partner you, Lou," he offered kindly.

"That would never do!" Louisa said with horror. "I could *not* have you beg for partners for me! It would be too humiliating."

"Can't see why, if you are so set on dancing,"

Tommy grumbled. "Lady Melinda is here. Perhaps if you chatted with her one of her young men would invite you to dance."

"Oh, Tommy!"

They had finally reached the alcove furnished with an ornate settee flanked by potted palms. Enthroned there was the Countess of Sitwell, her grandmother, attended by Lady Marie and Mrs. Lauderdale. Her expression was forbidding, enough to frighten off any potential partners. She eyed Louisa's gown through her lorgnette, sniffed loudly, then ordered Tommy to fetch her granddaughter a chair. Conversation ensued.

"Enjoying yourself, Louisa?"

"Yes, Grandmama, very much so."

"Can't think why you should be. Insipid sort of party. Too stiff and formal," the older woman grumbled.

Louisa was momentarily nonplussed. "All of Society is here," she finally murmured.

"You don't *look* like you're having fun," her grandmother said shrewdly. "*I* thought you were giving young Colville a scolding back there on the dance floor. Not that he doesn't deserve it, I'm sure."

Louisa squirmed uncomfortably.

"Mama! Louisa is very pleased and excited to be here. Aren't you, Louisa?" Lady Bardoff interposed.

"Yes, Mama."

"We have been planning for this for weeks!"

Lady Bardoff said happily. "What to wear, which jewelry would suit, how to arrange Louisa's hair, and Susan's too, of course. I spent many hours with the modiste deciding on Louisa's gown!"

The Countess looked at Louisa's dress with disgust, but refrained from commenting. Louisa wished that she could sink into the floor to escape this humiliating scene. How would she ever survive this evening? she asked herself miserably.

"My dearest Countess! I had no idea you were up from the country!" a masculine voice exclaimed with pleasure.

"Francis Geffrey, you young devil! What are you doing at a dull romp like this?" the countess asked, a gleam of amusement in her eyes. The party turned to the newcomer with relief.

"Certainly not dull! I am escorting my mother, who is enjoying the evening immensely. I must tell her that you, too, are here. She will enjoy seeing you, and the other ladies, after all these months." He bowed gracefully to Lady Bardoff and Mrs. Lauderdale, and finally to Louisa. "And it is a pleasure to see you again, Miss Bardoff," he said with perfect courtesy. "This is your first visit to Almack's Rooms, I believe?" he asked.

"Yes, my lord," Louisa answered shyly.

"I would be honored if you would join me for this dance, Miss Bardoff. If I have your permission, Lady Bardoff?"

As this lady nodded her beaming approval,

Louisa caught a glimpse of Tommy's face. His disgusted look communicated his opinion of damsels who poured out fears and trepidation of their evening's success, such as she had expressed a few moments before, only to have a positive Corinthian like Lord Geffrey standing up with them in a matter of minutes. This clearly laid to rest any possibility that Louisa would spend the evening with the matrons. With his responsibility over, Tommy beat a hasty retreat from the countess and the ladies and sought more congenial company.

Louisa and Lord Geffrey joined a set that was just forming and were soon moving to the music. To her suprise, Louisa found herself positively enjoying the dance, her fears of social failure banished from her mind.

"I see that your brother is attending Miss Lauderdale," Lord Geffrey said casually. "They make a handsome couple."

"Yes, many people say so! And some say that they should make a match of it. In fact, nearly everyone does."

"And who are the exceptions?" he asked with a smile.

"Why Susan and Ruston, of course!" she laughed back. "Such a thought has never entered their minds."

"But naturally. What seems obvious to those around them is not their view at all."

Louisa smiled back at him as the dance separated them. She thought of Ruston with affection. Honest, forthright, loyal, totally without guile, he was the kindest of souls and the best of all possible brothers. Perhaps a trifle sporting mad, but at least his tastes ran to pugilistic matches and cockfighting and a good fast gallop. He rarely plunged into gambling, and cards were declared to be a dead bore. No, Ruston preferred the country and its daytime activities of hunting and fishing and shooting to the Town's late night amusements. In fact, he disdained Town life, fashion and Society, and although two years older than Louisa, he was in many ways her junior. Some day he would take over the management of his family's estates, marry a young lady of good family, probably a neighbor's daughter, and raise a large brood of children.

The dance brought Lord Geffrey and Louisa back together again. "A pity they don't take to one another and make a match of it," Lord Geffrey said amiably.

"Whyever should they?" Louisa said with surprise.

"They know one another well, Susan is already familiar with the way of life he will lead, they have the affection of long friendship to sustain them. It would be a most sensible match."

"But surely there must be more to marriage than that!" Louisa said indignantly.

"More than a high regard for one another and a firm foundation for a happy life together? Many couples settle for less," Lord Geffrey answered with surprise.

"But, but . . ." Louisa began to argue, then was suddenly struck with the similarities of her own situation to Tommy's. A high regard, affection, loyalty, familiarity, were to be the basis of their marriage. Was she arguing against her own future? The thought made her blush.

"My lord, they are not so well suited. Susan requires the constant gentle attention and affection of someone who loves her. Ruston is far too bluff, forthright and hearty to provide that. Susan likes the Town, Ruston the country. There are far too many dissimilarities between the two of them to warrant a match," including the fact, she thought, that Susan was deeply in love with another man.

Lord Geffrey had seen her blush and cursed himself for his own tactless comments. For a man of address he had been singularly inept. Deftly, he changed the conversation to less distressing topics, recounting for Louisa's amusement a tale of a wind blown parasol and the efforts of several young gallants to retrieve it for its fair owner. Soon the music came to an end and Louisa was returned to her mother's side.

Lady Melinda and the Countess of Whitworth had joined the other ladies and were adding to the liveliness of the party. Soon Melinda was regaling Susan and Louisa with the latest *on dits* of who was flirting with whom, what a certain Lord S had sent

a young lady he admired, where so and so had pur-
chased that divine lace. Now in her second Season,
Lady Melinda was a knowledgeable fountain of
much innocent gossip. She was able to point out
well known members of Society whom Louisa and
Susan had not yet met and describe their fashions
and foibles. In the other corner of the alcove their
mothers were also gossiping, but about considerably less innocent subjects. In carefully lowered
tones they discussed Lady J's latest lover, which
royal duke had committed the most recent folly,
who was the natural father of young Lord P. A
constant stream of young men was calling Lady
Melinda, and often Susan and Louisa, too, to the
dance floor. Tommy and Ruston had put in but in-
frequent appearances, their conversation consisting
of grumbling and complaints that they had been
forced to wear such outrageous gear as knee
breeches and stockings, with occasional sporting
tales that Lady Melinda at least found amusing.

During a dance that found Louisa and Susan sitting alone, Susan seized the opportunity to discuss
with her friend the progress of their investigation.
Disappointed with how little had been achieved,
they could only agree to pin their hopes on
Tommy's visit to his grandmother. Susan then
broached another concern of hers.

"How is John, Louisa? I know that I saw him
but a few days ago, but I cannot bear not speaking

to him and being with him. Is he disheartened with our lack of progress?"

Louisa thought of the enthusiasm he had shown for his visit with Aunt Enderbie, but did not tell her friend about it. "He has thought of a final solution to the problem," she said cautiously.

"And what is that? Surely not elopement!" Susan said with shock and surprise, her voice rising somewhat.

"Shhh!" Louisa hissed. "No, no, not that. I am to ask my mother about it. We fear that she is the only one who knows the answer."

Susan stared at her friend, dumbfounded. "You would do that for me?" she whispered, greatly moved. The prospect of plain dealing with Lady Bardoff filled her with trepidation, that lady being given to grudges and bitter resentment when questioned on one of her opinions.

"Of course, dearest," Louisa answered bracingly, reflecting a courage she did not feel. "But we thought that we would be sure that there was no other way before I resort to it. It is our last alternative."

Susan nodded her agreement. "And it might make things worse," she murmured.

"It certain might," Louisa agreed.

"If only I could see John," her friend sighed.

"You really must not hope for that, at least not immediately. We must be very careful. We all agreed to it, no matter how difficult it might seem."

"I thought that I could be brave and strong about it, but I can't!"

Louisa shook her head no, trying to ignore the pleading tone in Susan's voice.

"Just to see him for a moment! I had hoped that he would be attending tonight," Susan added wistfully.

Louisa looked at her doubtfully. "You could not have spoken to him in any case."

"But just to see him!" Susan's face was tinged with pink, her eyes sparkling as she thought of her love. "Perhaps we could arrange something for Lady Alwell's ball later this week," she said hopefully, clutching her friend's hand.

"Tommy would not approve."

"But Tommy shall be in the country with his grandmother. He needn't know, at least not until after it is done!"

"I am not sure it would be wise!" Louisa protested feelingly. "We may forfeit all chance of bringing this to rights. And I dislike withholding anything from Tommy."

"John and I saw one another before!"

"That was when you were with me and John was with Tommy and we all just happened to meet. Anyone seeing us would not have connected your name with John's. If Tommy is out of town, they can't help but wonder, especially with the questions that we have been asking."

"*If* they see us. But we will arrange it in such a

way that no one shall! Those little rooms off the long hall leading to the ballroom would be ideal."

Louisa, who was vaguely familiar with the reputation enjoyed by that wing of Lady Alwell's house, was not at all sure that it was the thing to be seen there. After much argument, she allowed her friend to persuade her that the risk might be taken for the sake of the young couple's happiness. With some misgivings, she gave her friend her promise.

Only one other person had heard any of the conversation, and the part he did hear had been but a single word: elopement! Lord Geffrey had been approaching the alcove to ask for Louisa's hand in the next dance when he heard Susan's shocked exclamation. Surprised, he had stopped dead in his tracks, then a natural delicacy of mind had caused him to put aside his curiosity and retreat from what might be construed as a listening post behind the potted palms. But he was unable to stifle a feeling of unease that that single word had aroused within him.

Elopement?

VII

The morning of the glorious visit to Tattersall's arrived cold and damp, but Tommy Colville's spirits were high. He looked forward to a morning spent indulging his favorite interest, and in the company of a man he liked and admired.

John had been unable to accompany him, being in hot pursuit of yet another elderly relative who might provide assistance in the problem of the troublesome family feud. Louisa was urging them all to greater efforts, the specter of that last resort hanging over her head and Susan's tearful pleadings in her ears. Tommy's insistence that he approach his grandmother for information after the Tattersall's expedition met with indignant reproaches.

But all this was far from his thought as he hurried forward to greet his host. The older man was surrounded by the inner circle of the horse world. Pink with pleasure, Tommy found himself introduced to august members of the Four in Hand Club, certain tip-top goers, and a trainer who was acknowledged to be the best of his profession. All greeted him with pleasant courtesy, opening their ranks to him and deferring to his opinion on the one occasion when he was so sure of his ground that he had the courage to express it.

Lord Geffrey watched him with amusement, relieved that the youngster had better sense than to babble on with excitement. In all, Tommy was making a good impression on those present, and as his nominal sponsor in those circles Geffrey felt pleased. Young Colville listened to the men around him with suitable deference, his manners when spoken to were pleasing, his one judgment showing a naturally sound reasoning that was tempered with his knowledge of his own lack of experience. The contacts that Lord Geffrey was opening for the youth would stand him in good stead in the years to come.

The group broke up as a particularly controversial matched pair were brought forth. The animals were inspected jocularly, the more staid individuals commenting unfavorably on their withers and legs, the more flamboyant men praising the flash and spirit of the cattle. The Earl of Whitworth lingered near Lord Geffrey and his young guest, frankly curious about the burgeoning friendship.

"What do you think, Colville?" he asked amiably. "Would you lay down your blunt for them?" Lord Geffrey turned, waiting attentatively for the answer to the earl's question.

Tommy took one long last look at the pair, thought over his answer carefully, then shook his head in the negative. "No, I think not. They are a respectable pair, but not top-notch. Perhaps for a lady's carriage they would do, if she handled the ribbons with a firm hand. I suspect that their spirit has little backing it, and I doubt their staying power. A man would need a pair with greater endurance, but they would make a pretty enough show."

The earl considered this seriously, then added but one caveat. "The lady would need to have some skill with handling horses in order to manage them with any assurance of safety."

"But Colville has a point," Geffrey commented. "The spirit is mostly show and not substance, something easily subdued. After their freshness was run out of them, they would be docile enough."

The earl grinned good naturedly. "Well, they certainly won't do for Melinda. I don't know where she got it but she's taken a notion to having her own curricle. Can't say that I like the idea much, but it does no good to argue."

Tommy said admiringly. "At least she has some interest in it. Louisa doesn't know one thing about horses and frankly doesn't want to. I hate to say it but she looks for the ones with the pretty colors," he finished ruefully.

"Don't worry about it, Colville," Lord Whitworth said consolingly. "At least she won't break her neck."

"I thought she showed some aptitude for it when we had that discussion in the park," Lord Geffrey said with mild irritation as the other two men laughed.

"She won't recall any of it," Tommy scoffed. "It was your teasing way of explaining it that held her interest. She put it from her mind as soon as we sat down to tea."

Nettled, Lord Geffrey held his tongue with some difficulty. He suspected that Louisa was far more knowledgeable than she allowed Tommy to know. Her supposed ignorance was a foil for the young man's expertise, but her gentle teasing had shown an awareness of the niceties of good horseflesh, even if her experience was limited.

Smoothly, the earl intervened between the two younger men, pointing out the late appearance of one of the more eccentric gentleman of the turf. With an amusing anecdote he led the conversation into less controversial channels and soon had his friends laughing again. Peace established, he departed for his own engagements and Lord Geffrey and Tommy retired to the peer's club.

Over a satisfying nuncheon, the conversation followed an unexceptional course. A discussion of mounts led imperceptibly to the cavalry and Tommy's enthusiasm was obvious. He was familiar with the makeup of all the outstanding regiments, their mounts, famous battles and honored heroes. Lord Geffrey was treated to a dissertation on the superior tactical importance of the cavalry as opposed to infantry. Geffrey listened with amusement as his young friend gave him a panoramic view of the use of men and horses in warfare, carefully skimming over such disasters as Agincourt as being mere French blunders. Where modern cannon fit in he did not deign to say. When the flow had subsided, Geffrey sought a less exciting topic to discuss.

"Pity your friend Howorthy couldn't make it. He seems a sound young man. I would like to know more of him."

"John? John's the best friend I ever had. Up to anything, always ready for a lark, always there to help a chap out of a tight spot," Tommy said glowingly.

"I apprehend you were at Eton together?"

"Yes, we were in the same year. I never could get the hang of Latin and he used to nurse me through the exams. He'd sit up all night cramming with me."

Lord Geffrey chuckled, "Somehow I had formed the opinion that your activities together were less scholarly."

"Well, sir, we did slip out quite often for a bit of fun. Got into trouble for going off to see a bruising mill without permission. Same thing at Oxford. I only stood it a year, but we got into some fine scrapes. Smuggled a fighting cock into chapel once. You should have seen the uproar!" And with a shout of laughter he described the antics of the choirmaster, a personage familiar to Lord Geffrey from his own days at the university. The tale brought back memories of his own schoolyears that he had long since forgotten, and he grinned ruefully at the perennial foolishness of young men.

"If John hadn't thrown from the window the bag we'd used to smuggle it in, we'd have been caught for sure," he ended.

"You are fortunate to have such a friendship," Lord Geffrey said pleasantly.

"We have great times together. Or at least we usually do. Lately there has been all this fuss and bother." In his enthusiasm, Tommy forgot to be discreet. "Poor John is even threatening to elope, saying that he will carry her off wrapped up like Cleopatra in that rug. I suppose that love does that to you." Realizing that he had said too much,

Tommy broke off in confusion, then tried to cover his blunder.

"Sorry, sir, I never should have said that, John has grown much attatched to a young lady, a real brick of a girl, but his family and her family don't approve, and he's at his wits' end. I do hope, I mean to say I know that . . ."

"You needn't worry, Colville. You can rely on my discretion. I only hope that the couple can work out an honorable solution."

"Oh, well, Louisa says that we can work it out. We will see it clear in the end. She has us all running about on harebrained errands. She sent John off but this morning."

"Miss Bardoff did such a thing?" Lord Geffrey asked with surprise. Louisa's invovlement in what sounded like a clandestine love affair surprised him. He had thought that her nicety of manners would bar her from such a questionable enterprise. "And are you, too, assisting?" he asked dryly. "I am surprised that you are not hard at work on some errand for her."

"Oh, no! That wouldn't do at all. Besides, I had promised to accompany you today, and there was no way that I could be persuaded to break such an engagement! I will do what I promised for them, but there *are* limits!"

"Quite!" the other man said with confusion. He felt a pang of dismay and foreboding that there was something afoot, something highly suspicious, that involved Louisa, something which he didn't understand. He felt that he owed her a debt of gratitude for the kindness she had shown him; he suspected that it was due to her actions that his embarrassment had not been spread far and wide. He tried to tell himself sternly that this was none of his concern and avoided the temptation to seek more information from his young friend.

The conversation soon followed other channels. At least the reference to elopement was clear. Obviously Miss Lauderdale and young Howorthy were being driven to desperate straits, actions that failed to please the young lady if her tone of voice was any indication.

Young Colville attended to the time nearly an hour later, and with startled explanations and expressions of gratitude, he apologized for overstaying his welcome and took leave of his host. Lord Geffrey was well rewarded for his hospitality by the young man's sincere thanks and his praise and enthusiasm for all he had seen. He departed into a cold drizzle leaving his host behind with only his own thoughts for company.

VIII

Lord Geffrey soon encountered John Howorthy at
Lady Alwell's ball, an affair that had gathered most
of the *Haut Ton* under one roof. He was surprised
to learn that Tommy Colville had left town, but he
found time to pause for an amiable chat, his previous suspicions forgotten. Their conversation brought
a malicious jibe from one of Geffrey's contemporaries.

"Amusin' yourself with the Nursery Set, Geffrey?" he asked languidly.

"Hardly that, Scropes. Young Howorthy has long
since shaken its dust from his feet."

"Still a bit green, though," his acquaintance continued. "That waistcoat! And the cravat! What do
you suppose one should call such an arrangement?

Disarray? Chaos? It puts me in mind of his friend Colville."

Glancing pointedly at the other man's padded shoulders, Geffrey said shortly, "Those are minor mistakes that experience will set to right. A pity the same can't be said of everyone's errors of judgment."

His companion bristled, then saw fresh source of amusement. "At least Colville will be well suited to that Bardoff chit. Can't imagine how her mother can dress her that way. Makes a plain figure worse," he said arrogantly.

"Miss Bardoff is none the less a lady of gentle breeding and bearing, ever rarer attributes in these modern times!" And with a condescendingly slight bow, Lord Geffrey left the man and moved across the room to where Louisa stood by her mother.

"Are you perchance able to give me this dance, Miss Bardoff?" he asked formally, having bowed to Lady Bardoff.

"Thank you, my lord, but I do not waltz in public," Louisa said, her disappointment evident. Lady Bardoff, flattered by Lord Geffrey's attention, was suddenly thrown into a confusion. A patroness of Almack's had sanctioned Louisa's dancing the step with Tommy Colville, so just this once, perhaps . . .

"Well just this one time," the proud mama granted.

Before she could say more, Lord Geffrey had swept Louisa on to the dance floor. He smiled with satisfaction when he saw the look of amazement on Scropes' face, then tightened his arm around Louisa's waist and firmly whirled her away.

He was surprised to find her so light on her feet, and her height was also greater than he had expected, although she was still well below the level of his chin. He was finding it quite agreeable to whirl her across the floor and her expertise was sufficient that he felt safe to direct a few unexceptional remarks to her without endangering her mastery of the unfamiliar steps.

In fact, her poise was so remarkable that he was soon teasing her about it.

"For a young lady who does not waltz in public, you are doing remarkably well," he said.

Louisa glanced up at him and smiled. He noticed for the first time that she had a dimple near the right corner of her mouth, a dimple that gave an enchanting gaiety to her expression.

"I *have* had the opportunity to practice it with my brother Ruston. And I danced it the other night at Almack's Assembly with Tommy partnering me. Do I appear to be frightfully immodest, taking this all so calmly?"

"Scandalously so!"

"Perhaps I should blush," she suggested thoughtfully.

"Can you do that at will?" he asked, suddenly interested.

91

"No," she said sadly. "But I can hold my breath."

By now Lord Geffrey was having trouble remembering his own steps. He was shaking with laughter and more than once had to apologize for blundering into other couples. His frank enjoyment was drawing no little attention from the dancers around them, and several young men began to suspect that it might be worth their while to seek out Miss Bardoff for the next dance.

"Please don't do that," he finally gasped to Louisa through his laughter. "It might cause you to faint. That would be rather an extreme method of displaying your delicacy of mind and disapproval for something as shockingly fast as the waltz."

"True. And Mama would not approve."

He nodded in mock solemnity. "She would never allow you to stand up with me again."

Suddenly shy, Louisa said quietly, "That would never do!"

"No, not at all," Lord Geffrey agreed seriously, then he spun her even more skillfully around the floor.

For the rest of the evening Louisa was surprised to find herself sought out by young men not of her immediate set of friends. Not even the influence of Lady Melinda, who was not attending that evening, could explain it. Although she was flattered and inclined to enjoy the extravagance of standing up for every dance, it did interfere seriously with her plans. She had promised Susan and John that she would help them to arrange a meeting in one of the obscure little anterooms some distance from the crowd of the ballroom.

It was not until supper time that she was able to slip away, having signaled to the co-conspirators that the time was ripe. They made their separate ways through the throngs of laughing guests and were soon gathered at the door of the small, empty room.

"We must be quick about this," Louisa said anxiously as she glanced up and down the long hallway. "Mama will soon wonder at my absence from the meal."

"Just a few moments together," Susan said desperately. "We'll tell your mother that I tore my lace."

"Well, shoo, then. I'll stand guard out here."

As she stood her anxious vigil, Louisa wondered briefly what was passing between her friends. She felt a twinge of envy that they should share such a love. That she had never had a young man whisper gentle endearments into her ear was a source of growing discontentment to her. Susan's unhappiness over not seeing John, her blushes of pleasure when they discovered opportunities for meeting, all had moved her deeply, making plain the emptiness of her own life.

Louisa was a sensible young woman who appreciated the advantages of her proposed marriage to

Tommy Colville and the many undoubted virtues he possessed. He was kind, unselfish and easy going and would handle his future responsiblities with care and reliability. She was fond of him and knew that a life of comfort and respectability stretched out before her. For the first time there was a rebellious flicker of discontent in her heart.

A distant clock began to chime the hour and with a start she realized that some fifteen minutes had passed. She knocked softly on the door, then opened it.

"We must get back," she warned. The young lovers were sitting side by side on a small sofa, John's arm firmly around Susan's waist, her head on his shoulder. They looked up at her with surprise.

John glanced hastily at his pocket watch, then scrambled to his feet. "Good Lord! It hardly seems like it has been more than a minute or two."

"Must we go?" Susan asked, a pleading look on her face.

"Come dearest, it can't be helped at the moment," Louisa said briskly. "You go first, then I will follow, and then John will come."

Susan hurried down the hall after throwing one anxious, loving look over her shoulder. She disappeared toward the supper room. Waiting a few minutes, Louisa followed, then John close behind her. Louisa emerged from the long hallway flushed and anxious, casting a guilty glance around the not empty ballroom. She failed to notice a tall gentleman who was approaching the room from the adjacent conservatory. He stopped in surprise when he saw her expression and the direction from which she came, then tactfully stepped back into the shadows. Then John Howorthy appeared from the same hallway, hard on Louisa's heels, a similar look of apprehension on his face. He moved toward the supper room, leaving the gentleman with much to ponder.

Lord Geffrey had noticed Louisa's absence from the supper room and had gone in search of her. When the ballroom had failed to yield her, he had explored the conservatory. That place held no luck for him, either, and he had been momentarily stymied. That Louisa would go down the hallway in the direction of the smaller rooms never occurred to him. Most of Lady Alwell's guests rarely wandered so far, the area being best suited for clandestine meetings between lovers. The many anterooms offered an unusual degree of privacy for those who sought it, and its reputation was well established.

It was with considerable surprise that he had watched Louisa emerge from the wing of the house that had a certain notoriety. To see that John Howorthy was following her threw his mind into a turmoil of suspicion and shock. Could Louisa be playing fast and loose with Tommy Colville? And could she be doing it with his best friend. He was shocked with the very idea.

Heretofore he had admired Louisa for her

kindness and her lack of selfishness. Lord Geffrey had long since given up hope of meeting a young lady of fashion whose manners were as charmingly unaffected and natural as Louisa's were. Her small subterfuge with the torn flounce had amused him as he watched her skillfully lure her mother away from a scene that was potentially scandalous. He owed her his gratitude for not gossiping about his embarrassing encounter with Lady Melinda, or at least he suspected that he did. She had seemed to him to have a concern for other people that went far beyond her years, and was especially impressive in that she acted on them in such an adult manner. Whether dealing with a homesick French chef or the foolishness of those nearest and dearest to her, she had shown a poise and understanding that were admirable.

To now discover her involved in a secret meeting with a young man of whom her family disapproved, a young man who was her supposed fiance's best friend, was outrageous. Then the memory of his last conversation with young Colville struck him. Perhaps Lord Geffrey had misinterpreted the situation! Could it be that John Howorthy was in love with Louisa and not Susan? He may have read too much into that conversation in the park. And Tommy? Perhaps he, too, was aware of the intrigue. His comments on his friend's thwarted love affair suddenly fell into place. Could the young fool be aiding the lovers from a sense of deep friendship for

John Howorthy? This thought, which so neatly explained many questions, failed to ease the disgust he felt. And he doubted that a frank and open young man like Colville would countenance such a thing. At the very least, he would make clear the true relationship between himself and Louisa and put an end to the talk of marriage for the two of them.

Disappointment rose in him and he stifled it with a sharp oath. He was uncomfortably aware that his thoughts and speculations were swirling around in his mind without any rational control influencing them. What was he coming to? Louisa Bardoff was obviously a foolish chit of a girl, quite as unremarkable as any other schoolroom miss flung into her first Season too soon by over anxious parents. She was altogether beneath his contempt, and he would henceforth put an end to any and all association with her. Tommy Colville, a nice chap, had his sympathy.

And with that much settled, he stalked out of the conservatory, bade his hostess a punctilious farewell, and departed from the ball remarkably early.

IX

———•—◆—•———

Lord Geffrey's good resolve was sorely tried the next day when he answered a summons from Mrs. Enderbie, a formidable dowager with whom he was distantly connected. He had found her amusing in the past and had responded to the note demanding his presence with relief and amusement. Mrs. Enderbie could be relied on to take his mind off the disillusionment he had experienced.

Instead, he found himself seated by the same bow window that John Howorthy had occupied, though in a chair of considerably greater comfort. And to his surprise, Mrs. Enderbie was quizzing him about the actions of the very people he wished to ignore.

"I have made it my business to ask about, and I hear that you have been much in the company of my nephew John and his young friends," she said.

"I would hardly phrase it so strongly, madam." Lord Geffrey protested quickly. "I am barely acquainted with these young people. Your informers exaggerate."

"You ride with them in the park, join them for tea, take Tommy Colville to Tattersall's, sweep Louisa Bardoff off her feet with the waltz . . . That speaks of some time spent with them and familiarity gained," she said with asperity, irritated by the interruption.

"Just chance encounters, I assure you," Lord Geffrey answered quickly.

The old lady gave him a long considering look. "Nonsense. Giving young Colville lunch in your club was not a chance encounter. Now, I need the benefit of your observations. I *had* thought you to be a sensible man," she paused to glare at him coldly, "and I am unable to get about that much myself, so I rely on you to answer me frankly. I know that you will be discreet about what passes between us."

"Yes, madam," Lord Geffrey said with a sigh. His good manners were being taxed severely, but he managed to keep a composed expression on his face.

"John came to me with some mad scheme about patching up the quarrel between his mother and

Lady Bardoff. Not a bad idea, but his sudden interest in peace has me curious. After all, this silly feud
began before he was even born and has existed all
of his life. To my knowledge, he never took notice
of it one way or the other before. It doesn't make
sense."

"Perhaps he has reached the age of maturity
where he feels a responsibility toward his family
honor," Lord Geffrey suggested pompously.

"Harrumph!" Mrs. Enderbie snorted. "Stuff and
nonsense. He had some Banbury tale about his
parents needing to be invited to Louisa Bardoff's
wedding to Tommy Colville. Said it would stir a
scandal if his parents weren't at his best friend's
wedding. Mad!"

The mention of weddings left Lord Geffrey with
a cold sensation in the pit of his stomach. "A pretty
attention to the niceties, madam. Your nephew is a
young man whom you can be proud of."

"Bosh. He wants peace with the Bardoffs for
some other reason. You can't tell me that he cares
one whit what people think. He's nothing but an impudent young jackanapes, and there is more to this
than meets the eye."

"Some scheme he and Colville have dreamed
up," Lord Geffrey said with studied casualness.

"No, sir, I think not. Louisa is involved, too!"

"Oh?" he said faintly.

"Quite." Mrs. Enderbie glared at him, furious

that he was refusing to proffer the information that she so avidly sought.

"Well? Come, man, do be sensible. The only reason John could have for needing to be in Lady Bardoff's good graces is to court her daughter Louisa. Can you think of another?"

And in the confusion and turmoil of his emotions, Lord Geffrey could not.

"Surely to intrigue with young Howorthy behind the back of his best friend Colville is hardly the act of a gently reared young lady," he snapped angrily.

"Ah! Then there is something happening. Pish pash, don't be so foolish, man. Young Colville is in on it with them!"

"What?" Geffrey asked faintly.

"Of course. That young scallywag is galloping over to Bath to put his grandmother under his cross examination. They are all in it together."

Lord Geffrey stared at her, resentful that he must once again go over this sordid ground. At least this theory freed Louisa from the onus of deceit against Tommy. While he could not approve of her lack of frankness with her parents, he could sympathize with the plight of young love in the face of Lady Bardoff's arbitrary disapproval.

"Tommy and Louisa have never been more than fond of one another and no one has ever claimed otherwise. It was to be a nice, comfortable marriage of convenience uniting two neighboring families. But now sensible Louisa has fallen in love with young John!" Mrs. Enderbie explained dramatically.

The force of her conviction, coupled with what he had seen the previous evening, persuaded him that what she said was true. Although he would never betray to her Louisa's indiscretion of meeting with John surreptitiously, he was forced to acquiesce to her theory. Something of his quandary showed in his face, making his hostess wonder what was in his mind.

"Well, man, can it be?" she asked impatiently, frustrated by his unwillingness to commit himself.

"I have seen nothing that argues against your theory," he admitted cautiously.

Snorting again at his pomposity, his hostess pressed on. "So you believe it to be the case?"

In all honesty, Lord Gaffrey could only allow that now he did.

"Well, won't this be a spectacle!" Mrs. Enderbie said with satisfaction as she leaned back in her chair. "I wonder if the young people can bring it off. Any one of them has more native sense than their mothers combined. I hope that I will hear all the details. I must get young John to tell me. He can keep nothing a secret for very long."

Smiling ruefully, Lord Geffrey rose to leave. "Then perhaps you should offer them your assistance, as repayment in part for the show."

"I already have," she answered crisply. "But it is

going to be a formidable problem to solve. I don't quite see my way through it," she admitted.

"I feel certain that the combined ingenuity of the young people and your wisdom and experience will be equal to the task."

"Not Colville's wit, I hope," she said with a chuckle. "The boy's horse crazy. Nice enough youngster, but he ought to be serving in the cavalry."

"What Colville lacks in ingenuity he more than makes up in loyalty," Lord Geffrey commented defensively.

"That is certainly true. Who ever heard of helping your best friend make off with your fiancee?"

Lord Geffrey winced. "And perhaps when the other affair is settled he will have a chance at his cornetcy," he murmured, almost to himself.

Mrs. Enderbie looked at him curiously, surprised at the degree of promise his tone implied. "I rather think that he will," she agreed. It struck her that Lord Geffrey was planning to gallantly clean up as best he could the debris left in the wake of the headstrong lovers.

"Madam, your servant," and bowing himself out, Lord Geffrey left the room, promising himself to avoid the young people whom he had befriended and all their turmoil, with the possible exception of Tommy Colville. That he had so misjudged their innocence and honor rankled in him.

Behind him, Mrs. Enderbie said to an empty room, "Dear Lord, what a mess it all is. I do hope that this Louisa knows what she's about, or there will be more than one heart broken in the matter."

X

Lady Bardoff's ball in honor of Miss Louisa Bardoff, her eldest daughter, and Miss Susan Lauderdale, the daughter of her dearest friend, was scheduled for the middle of the Season. Lady Bardoff had disdained the scramble of an early affair, clearly stating by her action that Louisa, already unofficially attached to a young man of birth and fortune, had no need to resort to undue activity to attract the notice of Society. Louisa could afford to wait in leisure before gathering her friends about her for her formal presentation.

With a fair hope of giving a ball that would be the peak of the spring's activities, especially in view of Louisa's unexpected popularity since the Alwell affair, Lady Bardoff made her plans. She was blessed to have a fine town house at her disposal, one graced with a spacious ballroom that allowed her to give full bent to her ambitions when she compiled a guest list that included some five hundred persons. Every individual of consequence (except those with whom she was not on speaking terms, and the upstarts of whom Sir Harry disapproved) was invited, and Sally Jersey had been heard to comment in an offhanded manner at Almack's that she just might 'take in' the Bardoff affair. With such a hope, the ball had every chance of being a success.

The decor was a traditional one, Sir Harry insisting that the fine Adams ballroom needed no ridiculous festooning, so plans for an Arabian tent were scotched. But bank upon bank of exotic flowers were planned, many bottles of champagne dusted off, the chef had been preparing delicacies for weeks and they were well on their way toward a pleasant evening.

Louisa and Susan were to be dressed in the style deemed suitable by Lady Bardoff for young ladies in their first Season. The many flounces of tulle filled out Susan's slight figure and made her an ethereal angel in the midst of a hazy white cloud. This same style had an unfortunate effect on Louisa's appearance, but by dint of much persuasion from Louisa, Susan and even Mrs. Lauderdale, Louisa's gown had been simplified to a style more becoming to her plump figure. It's elegant straight lines, abetted by the secret purchase of a pair of slippers with unfashionably high heels, made Louisa the happiest she had felt about her attire for any ball.

Only the anxiety of John and Susan's problem, still unresolved, marred her pleasure in the coming event. All of their diligent inquiry, even Tommy's visit to his grandmother's had failed to yield results, and Louisa had vowed that after the ball she would resolutely question her mother, point blank, about the causes of the long standing quarrel with the Howorthy family. They had all agreed that to approach Lady Bardoff before this important event would probably ruin it, if not lead to its being cancelled.

The day of the ball was one of such excitement that Louisa's flushed face aroused little comment. Louisa herself put down her slight faintness to the bustle of activities. The hairdresser had arrived early in the afternoon to do their hair, then Mrs. Lauderdale found a slight flaw in Louisa's dress that required another fitting for the adjustment, and Lady Bardoff, her capable preparations already in effect, indulged in a last minute crisis of nerves, leaving Louisa to deal with whatever problems arose.

One such problem was Lord Colville's suggestion that her engagement to Tommy be formally announced at the ball. This good man had posted up from his retreat in the country to attend such a signal affair, and it seemed like a jolly good idea to get this detail seen to. Now was as good a time as any. His own household was for the moment in surprisingly good order (Louisa's French was certainly paying off). It was as ready as it would ever be for a suitable reception to follow the announcement. Besides, he had no desire to come up to Town again, not if he could avoid it.

Sir Harry could see no argument against the plan, his wish for a Season for Louisa now being met, and after a brief discussion with the young people, it was decided. The fathers retreated to their clubs to compose suitably witty and sentimental toasts to the happiness of the couple.

The ball more than met their highest expectations. The rooms were packed with the haughtiest of the *Ton,* even the gay and flighty types who frequented Carlton House gracing it with their presence. The Bardoff and Colville tribes were naturally out in force and even an occasional Howorthy appeared, Aunt Enderbie demanding to be taken by John after she heard a rumor of the engagement announcement. But the elite of that small circle of families who made up Society had come to fill their champagne glasses, brush shoulders with friends and relatives, and dance the night away. As the evening progressed Louisa stood up for every dance, feeling very gay and light-headed as she spun around the dance floor with partner after partner.

Lord Geffrey was there, unable to keep away despite his intentions, but he had clung to the edge of the ballroom, chatting amiably with the dowagers and matrons. A chance encounter with young Colville in the park had warned him of the coming announcement and he had cynically come to watch the farce. In his mind it was an example of yet more perfidy on Louisa's part as she swung from John back to Tommy.

Seeing that Louisa was on the far side of the floor from her mother, Lord Geffrey punctiliously approached his hostess with compliments and thanks. She preened proudly as they chatted about the distinguished company present, flattered with Geffrey's delicate hints that her own popularity was the sole cause of the evening's success. Lord Geffrey privately guessed that the lack of any other amusement that evening, coupled with the reputation of Sir Harry's prodigal hospitality, had been the major factors in the party's success. Had he but known it, he, too, had been an attraction. His assiduous attentions to Louisa and her friends had raised many eyebrows, and more people than Mr. Scropes had found the situation amusing.

He had planned to slip away from Lady Bardoff before Louisa's dance was finished and she was returned to her mother's side. He had no wish to meet and speak with her. To his surprise, he heard

Freddy Whipple, her partner, speak anxiously behind him, althought the music was still playing.

"Er, Lady Bardoff, ma'am, do forgive me for interrupting you, wouldn't dream of doing it ordinarily, of course, but you see, er, Louisa is indisposed. Could you see to her?"

Lady Bardoff glanced up in surprise, seeing first of all that Louisa was also escorted by John Howorthy, and then that her daughter's face was very flushed and feverish indeed. Her honest affection for her child momentarily banished all thoughts from her mind of her feud with John's mother; she was merely glad that he had been nearby to assist the sick girl.

"Bring her into the anteroom, there is a sofa there and a fire in the grate," Lord Geffrey said crisply, usurping Lady Bardoff's authority. This lady, instead of being offended, nodded her agreement gratefully, then hurried toward the door of that room.

"I'm so sorry, Mama," Louisa murmured. "I did not realize what was happening." Young Whipple was standing by in some confusion and Lord Geffrey stepped to her side.

"Don't talk so," he insisted. "We must get you comfortably settled in the other room and see what is to be done for you." He took her arm, nodding to John to assist him, and gently supported her out of the ballroom. Freddy Whipple trailed disconsolately behind them, unsure of what role to play.

Lady Bardoff had already ordered the sofa moved closer to the fire. Servants were bringing blankets and smelling salts and orders had been sent to the kitchen to fetch up a hot tissane. The two men led Louisa to the sofa and gently eased her down upon it. John helped her swing her feet up on to it and Lord Geffrey placed a pillow under her head.

"Mr. Whipple, go fetch Mrs. Lauderdale," Lady Bardoff ordered, and that young man quickly departed, relieved that someone had told him what to do.

Lady Bardoff then turned to her daughter. "Perhaps you have just over exerted yourself, dear. You have danced every dance, you know," she added anxiously as she arranged a fluffy blanket around Louisa's arms and shoulders.

Lord Geffrey, who had been half suspecting some sham designed to delay the engagement announcement, shook his head no. Even his cynicism disappeared when he had felt the warmth of Louisa's arm as he supported her from the ballroom.

"I fear that she is running a fever, Lady Bardoff," he warned her. "She is far too hot."

"How long have you been feeling ill, dear?" Lady Bardoff asked her anxiously.

"I haven't been feeling precisely ill, Mama," Louisa answered faintly. "There was just a certain feeling of light-headedness."

"She thought that it was from the excitement," John added hastily, forgetting his own position in Lady Bardoff's eyes in his concern.

Lady Bardoff frowned at him briefly, then dismissed him from her thoughts. "I suppose that we had best . . ." She interrupted herself. "Ah! Thank heavens you have come," she said as Mrs. Lauderdale entered the room.

That capable woman bustled to Louisa's side, gently pushing aside young Howorthy. She felt the girl's face, her expression growing worried as she realized how warm it was. Taking a handerchief from her pocket, she gently mopped the moisture from Louisa's brow.

"Have you sent for a hot drink, Marie?" she asked her friend over her shoulder.

"Yes, it is just coming."

"I fear that we must get her to bed." The expected cup arrived and Louisa was urged to sip its contents. Momentarily, she felt greatly refreshed.

"I feel rather better, Mama. I think that the spell is passing," she said hopefully.

Lord Geffrey shook his head doubtfully. "I would advise caution, Miss Bardoff. You may be very ill."

Sir Harry entered the room at this point.

"What's this all about? That young chap Whipple came to me with some tale of Louisa being violently ill. It can't be! She is never sick!

Lou, are you all right?" he asked her anxiously, peering into her face.

"I am much better, Papa" she said with a brave attempt at cheerfulness. "This hot drink has refreshed me remarkably. I am sure that I will be able to return to the ball in a few moments."

Instead of reassuring her parent, she only succeeded in adding to his concern. Her faint voice and too pink complexion told him that something was seriously wrong. He felt her forehead, then ordered briskly, "You are going right up to bed, young lady. I will take you to your room myself."

"But, Papa! The party . . ." Louisa protested.

"The party will go on without you. After all, it is also in Susan's honor."

"Susan would never dream of letting it continue," Mrs. Lauderdale protested firmly.

"But . . ." from Sir Harry.

"If you must end the party because I have left it, I won't leave it," Louisa said suddenly, a hint of determination in her voice.

Sir Harry seized the opportunity. "That settles it," he said quickly. "You are going to bed but the party will continue. Mrs. Lauderdale, be so good as to take Lady Marie's place. We are relying on you to act as hostess in our absence while we see Louisa to her room."

With a doubtful nod, that good lady did as she was bade and returned to the party.

"Howorthy?"

"Yes, sir."

"You are to go find Tommy and tell him that Louisa is ill. Then the two of you will explain to his parents what has happened. Give them my apologies for leaving the ballroom. And the engagement announcement must be put off, naturally."

"Of course, sir. I will find Tommy immediately," John promised as he left the room.

Somewhat awkwardly, but with infinite tenderness, Sir Harry wrapped a comforter around Louisa's shoulders. His wife stood by, wringing her hands anxiously but giving little assistance.

"Now, girl, we will get you to your room." He slipped an arm around her waist and lifted her to her feet. "Your bed must be turned down and warmed and we will send for Dr. Randall."

"I will have Martin see to it," Lady Bardoff said, leaving Louisa to her husband's care as she hurried off on the errand.

There were now only three people left in the once crowded room.

"I am so glad that you are here, Papa," Louisa whispered into his shoulder. "For a moment I was frightened."

"There, there, darling. It will all be fine." He led her slowly from the sofa, gently giving her his support. "Thank you for your assistance, Lord Geffrey. I will always be grateful for the kindness you have shown my daughter."

Touched by the older man's dignity and his obvious love for his daughter, Lord Geffrey could only bow to him in response. He felt guilty for his doubts and suspicions about Louisa.

Suddenly Louisa's cheeks turned an ugly red and she leaned heavily against her father. Sir Harry struggled to support this sudden extra weight but it was too much for his strength and he had to ease her down to the floor. Without pausing to think, Lord Geffrey moved to Louisa's side and deftly gathered her in his arms, lifting her from the ground.

"If you will show me the way, Sir Harry, I will carry her to her room," he said quickly.

"Of course, of course," his host said, flustered by his fear for Louisa's well being. "Thank Heaven you were here."

Gently cradling the nearly unconscious girl, Geffrey followed Sir Harry up the stairs. Louisa stirred only once, vaguely aware of who was holding her in his arms. Somehow comforted by his strength, she relaxed and subsided into a restful sleep.

Eight days later, Louisa was able to sit up in bed for a few brief moments. Her mother horrified by the severity of her daughter's illness had done most of the nursing herself, allowing only Mrs. Lauderdale to assist. Plans were made to retire to the country to allow her to recover in peace and quiet as soon as she was strong enough to travel. Lady Bardoff was still greatly concerned for her health, although the fever had abated. Louisa, who had lost much weight and showed little appetite, was growing alarmingly thin.

"You may sit up only a few minutes, dearest," her mother said affectionately. She was determined that nothing would distress the patient, and set about cheering her up with great determination and no little conversation.

"We have had such a shower of letters and poesies, Louisa. Everyone has shown the kindest regard for you. Tommy has stopped by every day, despite Lady Colville's fear that the infection was still contagious," she chatted as she fidgeted with the pillows. "Do try to sip some of this soup. Let me hold the spoon for you. There! You really must try to eat more."

Louisa allowed her mother to talk on, aware that she had been very frightened by the illness, but her continual fussing was very trying for the patient.

"I don't remember quite all of what happened," Louisa finally said, stopping the flow of inanities.

"You were dancing with Mr. Whipple when you felt ill. That John Howorthy was nearby and helped Mr. Whipple escort you to me."

"It was very kind of Mr. Howorthy to do so."

"Quite," Lady Bardoff sniffed. Then remembering that he *had* performed a gallant service for her daughter, she relented somewhat. "His actions were very creditable, I must allow."

118

"He is such a good friend of Tommy's," Louisa said cautiously.

"That is the only reason I allowed him to come to the ball!" Lady Marie said huffily. "That, coupled with Mrs. Enderbie's insistance. If she weren't the widow of your father's distant cousin, I would never have sent her an invitation."

"I think that John is quite a nice person," Louisa said firmly, diverting her mother from her stream of complaints.

"I cannot but agree that his behavior was unexceptional," her mother admitted. "Much more than I would have expected from the son of that woman!"

Louisa sighed faintly, suddenly tired. She had hoped that Lady Bardoff, in her present mood of affectionate concern, would tell her something about the quarrel with Lady Howorthy. This was not a propitious opening.

Lady Marie saw her daughter's sudden weariness. "Louisa, you must lie down. You are quite exhausted," she said anxiously. She hurried back to the bed to help the patient.

Once settled in a more comfortable position, Louisa took her mother's hand and held it tightly. Drowsiness was overcoming her and she knew that she must ask her question quickly.

"Mama, Tommy and I are quite fond of John Howorthy. It distresses us that there is such ill feeling between you and Lady Howorthy. Whatever is the cause of it?"

"That woman's conduct has left me no other choice!" Lady Marie said indignantly.

"Just what has she done, Mama?" Louisa asked in despair.

Her mother was preparing to scold her roundly for her impertinence, but the weakness of Louisa's voice caught her attention and she looked anxiously at her daughter.

"You must get some rest, darling. I should never have allowed you to sit up like this. You are far too weak still."

"But Mama, how can I rest?" Louisa asked tearfully. "Poor Tommy is quite distraught about it. John is his best friend."

"I suppose that that silly young man asked you to pry . . ." Lady Marie fumed.

Louisa wearily turned her face away, ashamed to let her mother see her tears.

"Lou, dear?" Lady Marie asked with concern.

"Yes, Mama," came the muffled reply.

Lady Marie stared at her, dismayed by the depths of Louisa's distress. "Darling, if you must know, it was the tapestry."

Louisa turned her head slowly toward her mother, a faint look of surprise on her face. "Tapestry?" she asked weakly. "What tapestry?"

"Yes. The one of Cleopatra being smuggled into Caesar's presence wrapped in a carpet. Lady

Howorthy, my godmother, and I spent many hours on it and it was to complete the set at the Hall. My godmother promised it to me, but that dreadful woman would not relinquish it! I waited for a decent interval after Godmother's death, and was even most kind and friendly to the new Lady Howorthy, but she selfishly refused to send me *my* tapestry. Such a want of delicacy! Such vulgar greed!"

Louisa tried to think all of this through, "Mama, did you ever ask her for it?"

"Ask her?" Lady Marie said indignantly. "I would never dream of begging for what is already mine!" She crossed her arms stubbornly in a stance that was all too familiar to her family.

"Oh, Mama! Perhaps she didn't know!" Louisa exclaimed weakly, unable to do more than stare at her parent in amazement. Such a simple thing as that! And with this last, comforting thought, she fell asleep.

XI

———•◆•———

The days following her mother's disclosures were frustrating ones for Louisa. To begin with, she was still helplessly weak, unable to do the smallest thing for herself. A cup of tea was too heavy, too cumbersome, too difficult to balance whenever she tried to lift it with her own hand. She relied on her mother and Mrs. Lauderdale, occasionally assisted by the housekeeper Mrs. Simmons, for every assistance. Plumping a pillow, straightening a rumpled coverlet, sitting up for a few moments, being fed, all were done by another hand.

There was also her isolation. Susan had been sent to visit the Countess Sitwell, her mother and Lady Bardoff deeming it wiser to remove her from possible contagion. This also placed the responsibility of amusing and chaperoning a young lady of fashion in other hands. The anxious concern of her nurses, while deeply appreciated, began to pall when unrelieved by more spirited company. All of her friends, even her brother Ruston and her father, were banned from the sickroom. Tommy faithfully sent a poesie every morning, but Lady Colville was nearly hysterical in her refusals to allow him to so much as enter the contaminated house. After only a few days, Louisa longed to be amused.

The doctors were another trial for the patient to bear. Lady Bardoff had naturally sought the most fashionable and expensive advice available in London, and a procession of doctors paraded through the sickroom, feeling her brow, taking her pulse, inspecting her tongue. It was all most wearisome, especially in view of the diagnosis. Each doctor announced, portentously, that she had suffered some violent fever of unknown origin and should be confined to her bed with a regimen of total rest and quiet until her strength returned. Their terminology differed in some slight respects, but the content of their reports was always the same.

It was only natural that these many small vexations were made worse by Louisa's overriding concern to get word to her friends of her discovery. She had found the solution to their problem, but how was she to tell them? Unable to write a word, speaking only with those people who were sure to be unsympathetic to the import of the message, Louisa was in a quandary. She even considered bribing a maid to bear the message, but that seemed like a dangerous chance to take. All of the servants, with only one or two exceptions, were up from the country and totally loyal to their mistress, however erratic she was on occasion.

The visits from the doctors ended only when Lady Bardoff, distressed by her daughter's thin looks, hit upon the scheme of removing her to the country. There, she foresaw that the wholesome country air and abundance of simple, healthy food would bring about a miracle for her slowly recuperating patient. One doctor was found to agree to this therapy as suitable for a convalescent, so that in the midst of her plans and schemes for getting word to John Howorthy, Louisa was snatched away.

And so the journey was made to Sir Harry's country seat outside London, using the countess's cumbersome but well sprung traveling coach and going in slow stages. A brief trip by post chaise, it took a full day of traveling to reach there, the party leaving before dawn. Louisa, the object of all this solicitude, doubted the effect of such a journey on her weakened constitution, but she somehow endured the rocking of the coach over rough roads and arrived at her childhood home merely exhausted.

Sir Harry had ridden on ahead to make the arrangements for their arrival, and Louisa was greeted by the upper servants, huddled anxiously in the hall, the group dominated by her old nanny. This faithful retainer was determined to take charge of her care. Lady Bardoff, wearied by her own efforts and the tiresome journey, gladly abdicated command and allowed her daughter to be placed in bed by Nanny.

The next morning marked the beginning of a steady stream of delicacies out of the Hall's kitchen and into the sickroom. To everyone's dismay, most of them were sent back barely touched. Louisa, whose enjoyment of food had once been so healthy, had lost her appetite. Her anxious mother and Nanny consulted over menus and dishes, hoping to strike on the right combination that would appeal to the girl's appetite, but she continued to lose weight. Even fresh strawberries sent from a neighbor's hothouse failed to tempt her.

Louisa rebelliously wondered at their concern. If a person were unable to move about, if in fact that person had absolutely nothing to catch her fancy, why should she feel hungry? There was no one to talk to, she was declared too weak to read to herself, and whenever someone else read aloud it was always from the dullest book imaginable. Really! Lady Bardoff's sole concern in the country was her gardens, and when she wasn't reading aloud to Louisa from some worthy but boring book of her own choosing, she was discussing her plans for them.

It was finally this interest that gave Louisa the opportunity to take the first small step toward communicating with John. Offering to assist in the planning for redoing a deserted quarry, one that Lady Marie visualized as a sunken garden, she was declared well enough to sit up in bed and take notes.

"We must have a waterfall leading down to a lovely little pool in the bottom. Yes, that's the very thing."

"Do be careful of flooding, Mama."

"And ferns planted around the pool, of course."

"The soil will need mulching."

"And we must have something that will reflect in the water, even in the winter."

"Perhaps birch trees. Their white bark would be lovely in the water's reflection. But it would take such a time to grow them."

Lady Bardoff stopped dead in her tracks, her wandering interest taken up by the problem of the birch trees. "We shall transplant them. From the woods near the Pepperidge Road," she declared. Louisa slipped the notes for the garden to one side, exposing a blank sheet of paper beneath them.

"Camelias, perhaps? They would be well protected from the wind in the bottom of the garden," Lady Marie said tentatively.

Louisa finished a sentence, then commented, "Perhaps we could build a wall, or improve the side of the quarry to make a sheltered sort of cove."

"On the north end. That will give them plenty of sunlight from the south."

"We will have to keep the birch trees well away, if you want them to have any sunlight at all," Louisa said dryly.

"It is so confusing. They should have plenty of warmth, which means sunlight, of course. But they are not to have too much sun."

"Pity."

"Perhaps rhododendrons. There are some lovely ones in Lady Frankfield's park. Her grandfather spent years developing different strains. Make a note to write to her about them." Louisa made several notes.

"A bed of lilies?"

"Near the pond."

"And a bridge. We must have a bridge."

Louisa looked up with surprise. "It is rather a small quarry, Mama. Will there be room enough for a bridge?"

Lady Bardoff looked at her absently. "You are right, dear. A tiny summer house near the pool will have to suffice. It will be quite romantic."

"A sylvan glade," Louisa said dryly.

Her mother nodded her head in vigorous assent. "The bridge will do, near the stream."

"What stream?" Louisa asked blankly.

"The one that will connect the two ponds on the other side of the park. I have noticed that they are on different levels. A stream between them will have a merry little waterfall. Not a steep one, mind you."

"The very thing."

"And there will be a waterfall in the quarry."

"Of course."

"Perhaps a bridge could span the quarry. Are you getting all of this down, dear?"

Louisa guiltily returned her attention to the papers on the portable writing desk in her lap. The note to John was thrust aside.

"And I would like one flower bed to have only masses of Michaelmas daisies. As many colors as possible."

"Michaelmas daisies," Louisa muttered as she wrote.

"They will be lovely in the autumn. And irises should be near the lilies and the ferns."

"Irises."

"And the path to the quarry shall have azaleas all along it. That will be delightful in the spring."

"Azaleas."

"And herbaceous borders."

"Herbaceous borders."

"Perhaps with a cherry tree or two behind the azaleas."

"Cherry tree."

"The wall in the quarry shall have plenty of thyme falling over it."

"Thyme."

"Purple thyme."

"Purple."

"And raised beds for alpines."

"Alpines."

"Raised beds."

"Daffodils."

"Daffodils?" Lady Bardoff asked with surprise, her stride broken by the change of momentum. "Daffodils! The very thing! But where?"

"Along the stream?" Louisa hazarded at random.

"Along the stream! With wild flowers and a grassy expanse."

"Wild flowers." Louisa paused to look at her jumble of notes. Somewhere along the way she had begun sketching little maps of the gardens, dashing down the flowers her mother designated and placing tiny arrows to indicate their appropriate location. It was all growing most confusing, with the stream rather too near the quarry for clarity. She hoped that the actual gardens fared better.

"I shall leave the rose garden as it is," Lady Bardoff said thoughtfully to herself.

"Good," Louisa said with relief.

"They were laid out by your great-great-grandmother with the assistance of Capability Brown."

Louisa judged that if half of what she had heard about her great-great-grandmother was true, Capability had had little opportunity to participate in the planning and laying out of the gardens, despite his fine reputation. Her great-great-grandmother had been a lady of decided opinions.

"Such a history should be respected."

"Of course," her daughter murmured,

"The maze will have to wait until next year. Much of the boxwood is in sad need of replacement. It will be quite an amusing challenge to rearrange the paths."

The mazes had been the plaything of a Jacobean ancestor, his arrangement remaining intact over the generations, until now. "Most amusing," Louisa said dryly. So much for history.

"We will eliminate several of those nasty little cul-de-sacs that people seem to wander into."

Which was what courting couples especially seemed to do. There had been a particularly embarrassing incident two summers before, involving a young lady visitor and an unusually handsome assistant gardener. In their own way, the mazes had a reputation that rivaled the little rooms of Lady Alwell's town mansion.

"The very thing," Louisa said primly.

Lady Bardoff suddenly remembered the time. "Louisa dearest. How could you let me prattle on so! You must be exhausted. Here, give me the desk." Louisa managed to hold on to the papers while the desk was snatched away. As her mother turned her back to place it on a nearby table, she thrust the note to John Howorthy under her bed clothes. The next moment she was able to hand to her mother the gardening notes with a smile. Lady Bardoff glanced over them.

"We shall certainly not have any flooding in the quarry, dear. A water garden is all very nice, but it isn't what I have in mind. Not at all. At least not this year."

"Yes, Mama," Louisa said meekly.

"You seem to be getting much stronger, despite your lack of appetite," Lady Marie said with pleasure.

"I feel much better. Perhaps I can begin corresponding with my friends?" she asked eagerly.

"The very thing. I will be glad to act as your secretary. You may begin dictating to me tomorrow."

"Yes, Mama," Louisa said, feeling much more subdued. That was not at all what she had in mind; Lady Marie would see the contents of all of her letters.

"You are still much too weak to do more than jot down notes, dearest," Lady Bardoff said gently.

"If only I had visitors. Someone to talk to who has been out and seen new faces."

"Susan is still busy in London, as she should be. She volunteered to come down with us, but this Season is vitally important to her, so of course I insisted that she do no such thing."

"Yes, Mama."

"I could have your brother Ruston come down for a visit. He could be persuaded to leave Town, I am sure."

Louisa sighed. A discussion of the latest pugilistic exhibition was not very attractive.

"And Lady Colville has such a dread of infection that she won't allow Tommy to come."

"Yes, Mama."

Lady Bardoff looked at her with concern. "I hear that Lord Geffrey is staying over at Pepperidge Park. If it would amuse you, I shall write to him over there and invite him to tea. Perhaps a half hour of sitting up in a chaise lounge will not wear you out."

"Oh, Mama!" Louisa said with excitement.

"In the ordinary way I would not permit a comparative stranger, a gentleman who is not a member of the family, to visit you now."

"Yes, Mama," Louisa said apprehensively.

"But he has shown such a particular concern for your health, sending frequent inquiries and even flowers. And he was of great assistance the night of the party." Here Louisa felt her color rising as she remembered being carried in his arms. "Most gallant! He has been all that is proper. I shall ask him for day after tomorrow."

"Yes, Mama!" her daughter said with real pleasure.

Seeing her daughter's smile, Lady Bardoff congratulated herself on her inspiration. "The very thing!"

XII

———◆———

"A most admirable plan for a garden," Lord Geffrey agreed solemnly.

"It will be just the thing," Lady Bardoff assured him. "I intend to have everything in it."

"Have you considered a Chinese temple? As a sort of summer house on the edge of the small lake?" he asked earnestly. "I know that I have but small knowledge of such things, but . . ."

"Chinese temple?" Lady Bardoff's face filled with wonder. *"Chinoiserie!* But of course!"

Louisa groaned under her breath.

"The Regent's Pavilion at Brighton has several oriental features that are considered most elegant by those who appreciate true beauty," their guest said innocently.

"A Chinese temple! What an inspired thought. Lord Geffrey, I must thank you for your suggestion. I will surely give you the credit for the crowning glory of my garden whenever I show it to my guests," she offered generously.

"Oh, no! It is you who inspired me, Lady Bardoff," he protested hastily. "*All* the credit is yours, I assure you. Please don't mention my name in the matter."

He caught a malicious gleam in Louisa's eye and quickly averted his face to hide his laughter. This visit had not been at all what he had expected it to be.

Lord Geffrey had fully intended to wash his hands of Miss Bardoff and her sordid affairs, rescued from scandal only by the severest misfortune of her sudden illness. His sympathy had been aroused by her misfortune, but the cold light of day had brought reason to the fore and he had set a sensible course of action, sending only two notes of inquiry and a bouquet of flowers to the Bardoff home. More he wouldn't do.

However, when he sorted through various invitations for visits to the country, he surprised himself be accepting one that would take him into the neighborhood of Sir Harry's country seat. He had been there some four days now, dutifully sending another note asking after Louisa's health, as any gentleman of breeding should. The invitation to come to tea was only to be expected, he supposed. That it mentioned that Louisa would be present, the very person he had sworn to avoid, was something he ignored. He had ridden over on a fine mount provided by his host and was greeted by Lady Bardoff on his arrival.

Surprisingly, a tour of the quarry ensued. To his bewildered amazement, the good lady led him on a trek through a nearby woods, in order to point out the fine prospect provided by the quarry in its midst. In a cold, blustery wind, he heard Lady Bardoff describe the alpine plantings, cherry trees, camelias, and, oh, yes, the Michaelmas daisies, that she planned for the spot. He demurred only at the mention of the waterfall and pool, a small lake really, that were to grace it.

"But what about flooding?"

"Oh, heavens, no, Lord Geffrey. I don't want a water garden. No, not at all," his hostess had said briskly. He meekly accepted this answer and she turned to the question of the azaleas.

He was considerably chilled by the time they returned to the house, and the hot tea and cakes were most welcome. A large fire had been built up in the salon, for which he had Louisa to thank, and a comfortable chair set by the fire for his use. The talk of landscape gardening continued. Louisa, swathed in shawls, was already in a nearby chair.

"We are fortunate to have a bit of a ruin but a

mile from the house, Lord Geffrey," Lady Bardoff said happily. "It was once part of a castle, I understand."

"Actually a farmhouse, Mama," her daughter corrected.

"Well, a fortified one then. Why else use the stone? In the part of the world where I was raised, farmhouses were of wooden frames and shingles," she said tartly, ignoring the presence of the quarry she had lately been praising.

"Your ruin sounds most Gothic," Lord Geffrey said hastily. "It will be quite romantic to visit the spot when the weather is improved."

"Yes. I expect that it is as fine as Lady Westark's," she answered complacently. "Her ruin is reputed to have the finest Gothic atmosphere in the county, but I am certain that mine quite rivals it."

Congratulating himself on having avoided *that* point of interest on his tour that day, Lord Geffrey carried on the thread of the conversation. "As we have mentioned Gothic, have you read Mrs. Radcliffe's tales? *The Mysteries of Udolpho* is said to be quite enthralling, although I have never attempted to read it myself." Instead of striking the responsive cord he sought, he stirred Lady Bardoff's wrath. How was he to know that the trend of popular reading then current had become one of her pet peeves?

"I would not allow such material into my house,

sir, I assure you!" Lady Bardoff said indignantly. "The frivolity of it, the silly nonsense that it instills in the heads of the innocent, impressionable young people who read it are but two of my reasons for abhorring it. People should read improving books, works that provide information and stimulate the intellect!"

Lord Geffrey stared at her in surprise. Somehow he had not associated intellectual activities with Lady Bardoff.

"But Mama," Louisa said hastily, trying to soften her mother's rudeness, "many ladies do not object to the tales. One must read them knowing that they are not to be taken seriously."

"Precisely my point! If one is not to take them seriously, why read them at all? Louisa and I have been sharing some more worthy reading, Lord Geffrey. Several fine biographies and a history of the Bardoff family, written by a cousin of Sir Harry's, have been most informative and enlightening."

"Most worthy," Lord Geffrey said politely. He could not be offended by Lady Bardoff's outburst, it was such arrant nonsense. The good lady had already been instilled with the frivolity and fancies of the Gothic movement, despite never having looked between the covers of one of the many novels available. Poor Louisa must have been having a rough time of it with such worthwhile reading! He toyed with the idea of introducing poetry into the conversation, but feared that the reputation of poets had been forever besmirched by Lord Byron's affair with Lady Caroline Lamb. No, poetry was definitely not a good subject of conversation in the present company.

Suddenly Lady Bardoff exclaimed. "How foolish of me! Louisa, dear, you look to be quite exhausted. All this talk has quite worn you out. I have selfishly allowed my own pleasure in Lord Geffrey's company to lead me to neglect your health. We must have Willis take you upstairs immediately."

"Mama, I am quite comfortable here," Louisa pleaded. "To have company is such a pleasure! It is by far the best tonic for me that any doctor could prescribe."

"I dare say. You have eaten quite more than usual, which is all to the good, but you are still quite weak. Lord Geffrey, if you will forgive this interruption, I will see my daughter comfortably established in her own room."

"Of course. Allow me to assist in any way that I can," Lord Geffrey promptly offered.

Louisa blushed, remembering his strong arms carrying her the night of her party. To have Willis, the strongest man in the household, carry her upstairs with such a memory lingering in her mind was more than she could tolerate.

"Please, Mama, I will be able to walk, if you but give me your arm." Louisa stood up slowly, several shawls falling away to reveal how pitifully thin she had become as compared to her former self. Lord

Geffrey, shocked by her appearance, leaped forward to offer her his arm to lean on.

"You must have greater care, Miss Bardoff," he said warmly. Before Louisa could reply, Willis the footman had answered the bell and with him and her mother on either side to support her, she was led from the room.

Lord Geffrey waited patiently for his hostess's return. He was detained some few minutes longer by her talk of Louisa's health, talk that he encouraged. The extent of Louisa's illness was underscored yet again with these tales of the horrid discomfort and danger she had endured, and she earned all his sympathy. Lady Bardoff's silliness, even Louisa's suspected perfidy, all faded from his mind. Any misgivings that he had entertained toward the visit disappeared and he congratulated himself that he had had the good sense to come.

As Lady Bardoff's descriptions of her daughter's sickness began to repeat themselves, he made courteous motions to depart. He reached the front door with his hostess after hearing several more details, giving his thanks for their hospitality and offering his wishes for Louisa's speedy recovery.

"It is a pity that Sir Harry was not here to greet you, Lord Geffrey. He was called away but yesterday morning and will be distressed that you came in his absence. He has expressed the highest regard for you. It was to meet people of your stature that he insisted that Louisa have her Season."

Lord Geffrey, who had a high regard for Sir Harry's bluff, common sense, was duly honored. "I too regret that I was unable to see him. I have the highest opinion of his worth."

"He is a most sensible man," his wife said fondly. "Now let me call a footman to lead you to the stables. Or shall I have your horse brought to the door?"

"Madam, please don't trouble yourself on my account. I shall walk down to the stables, quite alone," Lord Geffrey protested with a smile.

"But, no, sir! That would be most shabby of me to allow such a thing," Lady Bardoff exclaimed.

"Not at all. And I thank you again for you hospitality." With a bow, he left her, taking the narrow gravel path that led around the house toward the stables in the rear.

He had turned the corner of the wing, when his attention was arrested by a hissing sound.

"Lord Geffrey! Psssst! Lord Geffrey!"

He glanced around, then perceiving that the sound came from above, looked up to see a pale face peering down at him from an open window.

"Thank Heavens that I caught your attention. I must beg a favor of you, sir, a most secret and urgent one. You are my only hope!" Louisa said piercingly.

Lord Geffrey was bewildered and concerned. "Louisa, I mean, Miss Bardoff, you should not be out of your room. You are far too ill to be up and about. Let me call someone to assist you back to your room." He turned as if to return to the front of the house.

"No, no, no! Heavens, I am quite able to walk, I assure you. You mustn't pay such attention to Mama and her fussing. I have a most important errand for you to carry out, if you will be so good as to help me."

Lord Geffrey was now suspicious of the clandestine nature of the encounter and his concern for the young lady's health was dimming fast.

"Any service that I may perform I will do so willingly," he said coolly, his manner belying the import of his words.

Louisa was delighted. "Thank you, my lord! I knew that I could rely on you." In her enthusiasm she was impervious to his obvious distaste.

Her head disappeared into the room, then popped out again. "Here is a letter. It is most important that it reach John Howorthy. I believe him to be in London yet." She tossed the heavily sealed missive from the window and it tumbled to the ground at Lord Geffrey's feet.

Amazed, he leaned over and picked it up. Anger rose in him when he realized that he had been cajoled into performing such a shabby task. A clandestine love note! A correspondence obviously unauthorized by her parents! And for a man such as he to be asked to act as carrier! He turned it over in his hands, his face averted so that Louisa could not see his expression.

"Such a silly thing it is about, but so important," she whispered down to him. "I could not even send it by mail, it would surely come to my mother's attention if I did."

He glanced up at her, a supercilious sneer on his face hiding his hurt and confusion. "Then by all means I must deliver it at once, Miss Bardoff." He flourished her a bow, bending deeply at the waist and even removing his hat.

Louisa was startled by his sudden change of attitude. She gaped down at his bent back in bewilderment, then snapped her mouth shut. How silly men were! One minute he was all tender concern for her well being, expressing sympathy and kindness, even warmth, and the next he was sneering!

"I trust that I am not inconveniencing you, sir!" she said haughtily, momentarily forgetting that he was her only hope for getting the vital note delivered quickly.

"Not at all, Miss Bardoff," Lord Geffrey answered sardonically. "I frequently carry such billets. Your note is quite safe with me, I assure you."

Louisa looked down at him with exasperation. What had taken possession of the man?

"Then I *shall* rely on you," she answered pointedly. She pulled her head in from the open air and slammed the window sash down, disregarding the noise it made.

Lord Geffrey stared angrily at the closed window. After one more sarcastic salute at the blank glass of its panes, he crammed his hat back on his head and stalked down the path to the stable. His look was so foreboding that the groom who had cared for his horse gave up all hope of a tip, counting himself lucky if he were to escape a tongue-lashing. Instead, Lord Geffrey tossed him a half crown, the first coin his fingers encountered in his purse, then turned and galloped away toward his host's home.

XIII

By the time he had reached his host's home, Lord Geffrey had galloped off much of his anger, but his disgust and contempt remained. He was furious with himself for becoming involved with such a shabby affair, and resolved to end his remaining part in it as quickly as possible. With as calm a manner as he could muster, he offered his thanks to his host, proffered some passable explanation for his hasty departure, and prepared to leave for Town. Messages were sent ahead for horses and his valet and groom were alerted.

The next day dawned clear and cold and he set out in his private chaise for London. A sleepless night had done little to revive his spirits and his two servants dealt with him warily. The groom, who accompanied him on the road, had been with His Lordship's family for many years and was bewildered by his master's unwarranted ferocity. The horses were driven skillfully but pushed to within a hair's breath of their limit. The man had never seen Lord Geffrey in such a state and feared that the cattle would soon be winded. In this he underestimated his master's ability and self control. Even in his present state of mind, Lord Geffrey could not bear to mishandle his horses, or any one else's for that matter. Only the slight mischance of a loose wheel prevented them from reaching London in record time.

They arrived at Park Lane in the afternoon. Instead of resting from his long journey, or adjourning to his club, Lord Geffrey flung himself into a fury of activity. A quick trip alone to an undisclosed spot seemed to bring him no satisfaction, but instead goaded him into a flurry of note writing and message sending. The groom watched from the stables and the household's kitchen, following the activity as best he could and seeking some reason for it.

When the Dowager Lady Geffrey, who also found her son's unusual occupations disturbing, sought information, she naturally sent for the groom. He was brought into her small, private parlor, hat in hand, fully aware of the cause for his summons.

"Samuel, I trust that you and your family are in good health?" Lady Geffrey asked kindly.

"Very good, ma'am."

"Your youngest. Has her cold quite passed?"

"Yes, m'lady."

"And the trip you have just returned from was a pleasant and uneventful one, I hope?"

"To all appearances, m'lady."

"But it seems to have had some effect on my son, Samuel. I do not understand his sudden quitting of the country. But a few days ago he wished for nothing but the chance to leave Town. Now he has returned to it."

Samuel's attitude had subtly changed. Although he had spent all of his life in the Geffrey family's service, he was ill-accustomed to dealing with a lady sitting in a silk covered chair in a fine parlor. The stable was his natural surroundings. But they had now reached the crux of their conversation and his stilted courtesy toward his social superior, so firmly drilled into him by his wife, slipped away as he considered the problem at hand.

"I canna explain it, ma'am. He were fine until yesterday, as fine as he's been this time past."

Lady Geffrey nodded her understanding. Her son's restlessness over the last few months had not escaped her attention. His courtship of Lady Melinda had given her a clue to his needs, but when this had come to naught she had shrugged philosophically and put off hopes of a grandchild for the time being. And the sudden aversion to his usual pastimes of cards, drinking, and dubious women, which had accompanied this mood, was all to the good. She had hoped that the visit with his old school friend would soothe him, but apparently it had done just the opposite.

"And what took place yesterday, Samuel?"

"He went visitin'. To Sir Harry Bardoff's Hall. 'Tis but a niceish property near where His Lordship were stayin'."

"Yes. I know it well," Lady Geffrey said faintly. Now what could have taken her fastidious son there? Surely not Lady Marie and her chatter, and Sir Harry had been seen about London on business this week. Who then? Louisa? But she was certainly not a type her son usually sought out, and she was reported to be still convalescing from that sudden illness. Although her son's strange behavior of late made it impossible to rule out this possibility, she strongly doubted that he had formed an attachment for Miss Bardoff.

Resolving to find out more of the Bardoff family's business, she dismissed Samuel and began to put her own plans into motion. The groom, relieved that the problem was now in authoratative hands, left the parlor with a lighter heart.

Meanwhile Lord Geffrey had met with some success. John Howorthy had been reported returned to his parent's home in Cavendish Square, and he seized the opportunity to relinquish the letter, and his responsibility, immediately. The meeting proved to be even worse than he had expected it to be.

John was surprised when Lord Geffrey was announced. To begin with, this gentleman was more a friend of Tommy Colville and Louisa. This was the first occasion when John had seen him privately without one or the other of his friends being present. And then, the hour was a deuced awkward one. John would have been at Brooke's laying his wagers down on the baize, if it weren't for an unfortunate mud puddle and a fool of a hackney driver who had splashed him from head to foot in passing. Instead, he had been forced to pass by his home and change into clean attire. And now, here was a visitor! Perhaps Tommy had sent him with a message? Damned unlikely.

"Lord Geffrey, good to see you, sir!" he said cordially as his good manners demanded. "May I offer you a glass of wine? Some Madeira?" His guest's manner further added to his confusion.

"Mrs. Howorthy. Good of you to see me at such an hour," Geffrey said coolly after he had executed a punctilious bow. He had not forfeited his hat and driving coat to the footman in the hall, and looked formidable and huge to young John. "I am here on an errand for a mutual friend of ours."

"Quite, quite!" John said, his confusion only mounting as he compared such a friendly gesture with Lord Geffrey's formal manner. My God! It couldn't have to do with a duel, could it? He edged toward some chairs. "Shall we, uh, sit . . . ?"

"I can linger only a few minutes, sir. Once my mission is accomplished I shall go my own way." And it's about time, the older man thought to himself angrily. He removed his gloves and tossed them negligently on a nearby table, then delved into the pocket of his many-caped coat.

"Miss Bardoff asked me to see that you got this with all possible speed. She assured me that it was most important."

"Louisa?" John was momentarily dumbfounded. An important note from Louisa could mean only one thing, the success or failure of their efforts to find the reason behind their mothers' long standing quarrel. Here was the key to all of his future happiness!

"Excuse me, sir," he said eagerly, snatching up the note, much to Lord Geffrey's disgust. Forgetting his manners, the young man ripped open the seal and read its contents quickly, a look of surprise spreading over his face.

"Dash it all, Cleopatra's Carpet! Who would have thought . . . ? How simple it all is!" He stood staring at the note for some moments, smiling happily to himself.

His guest, who had made no comment thus far, stared at him with contempt. Impudent young pup, planning a young woman's ruin, smiling cheerfully while an innocent young girl compromised herself with an illicit love note. And the reference to Cleopatra's Carpet! Surely these youngsters weren't planning to smuggle someone into . . . Into where? Or perhaps they were going to smuggle someone *out* of somewhere!

John had finally put down the letter, then snatched it up as he was hit by the thought of his mother seeing it at this juncture. He thrust it into his coat pocket instead. "Sir, thank you, sir. You have been the greatest help to us! Some day we will be able to tell you just how much and perhaps even begin to thank you properly for all you've done." In his enthusiasm he failed to notice the look of disgust on the other man's face, a look that spoke volumes.

In any case, Lord Geffrey left immediately to seek out the distractions of one of the more notorious gaming hells in Pall Mall. While Howorthy planned his dash to his father's country seat on the morrow, Lord Geffrey tried to drown his disgust with strong spirits and deep plunging at the tables. His cronies greeted him affectionately after so long an absence and he found himself returning to the habits of the worst of them.

Surprisingly, Lord Geffrey awoke early the morning after his debauch. An iron constitution had saved him from the worst effects of his indulgences of the previous evening, but he had been unable to forget the events that had triggered them. The shock of Louisa's duplicity was still with him.

That he could be such a bad judge of character infuriated him. He had enjoyed Louisa's company, her humor, and her kindness, her fun-loving disposition, but mostly her apparent good sense. The conviction that this was no silly miss had caused him to lower more barriers than he had realized at the time and admit her to his friendship as one of the rare women to enjoy that status. He had refrained from the intense and insincere flattery and devotion that most women seemed to expect of any man and had allowed himself to indulge in something altogether happier and more satisfying. Louisa was the antithesis of all the Society ladies, experienced and inexperienced, whom he had learned to distrust. Or so he had thought.

The savagery of his denunciation was overclouded by a feeling of concern. Whatever the young people were planning, Louisa would be too weak for many days to be able to even leave her home, much less take on a long and hazardous journey. The memory of her drawn looks worried him despite his efforts to thrust it aside. She needed peace and rest in which to recuperate. But what was all this urgency about? Surely they would have the sense to postpone their damned elopement.

His worry goaded him out of his bed and to the bell to call for his valet. Whatever the right or wrong of the case, he appeared to be the only person of sense and judgment aware of what was going on. Despite his promise to Louisa and Tommy to keep silent, and the resolve to withdraw that he had made to himself, he must discover what was afoot and talk some sense into these foolish children. To the amazement of his valet, who was aware of the hour of his return the night before, he was dressed and out of the door well before nine o'clock in the morning, off on yet another of his incomprehensible errands.

He arrived at the Howorthy home too late. The butler informed him that the young master had departed for his family's country seat early that morning, in fact before dawn. Further inquiry revealed that he had taken his own chaise, pulled by only a pair of horses. Geffrey heaved a sigh of relief at this last information. With only two horses in harness, the young man could not travel that fast. There was still a chance of reaching him before anything irreversible had been done. And the question of which road to take to follow was easily answered. Although Lord Geffrey doubted that tale of a visit to his parent's country home, the Howorthy estates lay near the Bardoff's. He hoped to catch young Howorthy before he reached either place.

His valet had a second shock that morning. Lord Geffrey returned home, stripped off his impeccable coat and pantaloons, and demanded his buckskins and riding coat. Before noon, he had set out on horseback for an unknown destination. By this time, the staff in the Geffrey town house were beside themselves with curiosity and concern.

After several hours of hard riding, Lord Geffrey was approaching the neighborhood he sought. Information he had gotten at posting inns along the way told him that his quarry was not far ahead. Unfortunately, no one could tell him which road to take when he reached the critical fork. He knew that the right turn led to Howorthy Hill, the left to Bardoff Hall. Should he go left to the Bardoffs' home, thus guaranteeing an eventual encounter, or should he gamble and try to reach John near his parents' home before this foolishness got any further?

A faint cloud of dust decided him. Although he was sure that the Bardoffs' place was the young man's destination, the opportunity to end the affair before it reached the point of open scandal, coupled with this faint trail, caused him to take the right fork. He was soon on the carriage drive leading up a gentle slope to the Hill. With any luck the Bardoffs would never know what their daughter was planning.

The many bushes filling the park would have displeased Lady Bardoff with their wild, untidy appearance, but they afforded excellent camouflage for Lord Geffrey. Dismounting, he tied his horse to a tree and approached the house on foot until he had an excellent view of the front door.

John Howorthy's carriage stood before it, the

horses' heads being held by a stable lad. From the house there emerged a curious sight. Two men, one of them young Howorthy, were carrying a giant roll of material. They heaved it into the carriage and Howorthy scrambled onto the box and took up the reins. With a merry flourish of his whip, he started down the driveway.

Lord Geffrey ran to where his horse was tethered and after a few moments was galloping off after his quarry. What in the world was that carpet for? That it was a carpet he was sure, his mind casting back to the strange conversation he had had with Tommy Colville after their visit to Tattersall's, and then there were the words that Howorthy had murmured as he read the letter from Louisa. It had been haunting him for some time. But what the devil did this young fool plan to do with a carpet? Wrap Louisa up in it and carry her out of the front door? Hide her under it in his carriage? Smuggle her into his parents' house in its folds? Thrown off his stride by his wild surmises, Lord Geffrey was unsure of his next move.

He hesitated too long, for he suddenly lost the initiative. Howorthy had turned down a little used country lane that proved to be a short cut that led them unexpectedly to within sight of Bardoff Hall. Lord Geffrey discovered that he had waited too late. His quarry had pulled up at the front door, knocked on it, and then quickly disappeared inside. Howorthy had walked straight into the lion's den!

Geffrey waited in an agony of suspense, shivering with the cold of the late afternoon. In the hastening twilight, he was just able to make out that the carriage had been left undisturbed in the driveway. No furtive figure had crept past the lad at the horses' heads and into the chaise.

Suddenly the front door was thrown wide open and a group of people descended toward the carriage. Lord Geffrey recognized Lady Bardoff at their head, and to his surprise, she was clinging to John Howorthy's arm, a happy smile on her face. The two footmen lifted the roll of material from the chaise and carried it past Lady Bardoff and into the house. Her happy laugh trilled out in the gloom as she lead her guest back inside. Once again the door closed.

The watcher in the bushes was bewildered. That night was falling was fortunate, for the bushes barely hid him they were so well trimmed. In his chilly retreat, Lord Geffrey recounted the day's events to himself. John Howorthy had left Town in haste to deliver a carpet, presumably an aid for elopement with Louisa Bardoff, into the hands of Lady Bardoff, Louisa's mother and his own mother's worst enemy. And Lady Bardoff had greeted this seducer with hospitality, even pleasure. Her footmen had removed the carpet from the carriage into her home for him. Even if she were ignorant of the plans for the carpet, why was she being so cordial to a declared enemy of her family? And why carry the carpet inside? Baffled and unhappy, Lord Geffrey decided that the only thing left to do was to wait and see it through. He settled in as comfortably as he could.

Some forty minutes later, Howorthy reappeared at the door. His horses had been patiently led up and down the driveway by the lad and all was ready for his departure. He bowed gallantly over Lady Bardoff's hand, received an affectionate pat on the cheek from the lady, and was soon moving cautiously down the moonlit driveway. Lord Geffrey moved stiffly toward his own neglected mount and followed after him yet a little farther.

As he suspected, Mr. Howorthy took the short cut back to the comfort of his parents' home, apparently alone. No small figure was smuggled out of the carriage and into the house. On the contrary, Howorthy leaped down, tossed the reins toward the approaching groom, and raced up the steps two at a time. The front door opened in a blaze of light and admitted him into his home.

Lord Geffrey was less fortunate. He turned his weary horse toward the London road and began the long ride to the nearest inn, which was several miles away. Already distressed by the certainty that he had made an embarrassing mistake, how he didn't know, his discomfort was further increased by a light drizzle that soaked through his coat. Soon his only thought was for a cup of warm punch, a fire and hot food. He hoped that the stables of the inn would be warm and comfortable. His horse too needed comfort. The lord knew that with his patience and endurance he had shown to better advantage that day than his foolish master.

XIV

————◆·◆————

No one quite understood how John had managed to explain it all to the two ladies, least of all John himself. His later descriptions of his actions were sketchy indeed.

Louisa always suspected that her mother, delighted with the return of 'her' tapestry and more than a little reconciled to begin with after John's kindness toward her daughter that hideous night of the party, had simply not expected it. She had won her point, after all. The tapestry was now hers. And she had been saved the painful necessity of explaining to her incredulous family and friends how the feud had all begun.

Lady Bardoff had treated the long lost tapestry

with loving care. It had been spread out in her sewing room and carefully inspected, an occasional broken stitch reworked. Louisa had grumbled that it wasn't a tapestry at all, they were woven after all, but her mother's good humor was such that she ignored this backbiting with a smile. Even the signs of dirt and neglect that she found failed to upset her. She simply sponged them away, using her undoubted skill, until the needlework looked as good as new.

It was then hung in its place of honor, between the other two scenes from Cleopatra's life, in the main hall of her husband's country seat. There, in that part of the building that had been constructed in the beginning of Elizabeth's reign, and later graced with a visit from that great queen, went the tapestries. That their mock classical theme and curious design and workmanship were ill-fitted to the exposed beams and linen-panel oak of the Tudor room bothered her not at all. She had even considered covering a finely carved panel that displayed the coat of arms of the first Bardoff baronet, but here Sir Harry indignantly intervened. At his insistence, the panel remained uncovered and intact. Lady Marie had suggested that they remove the piece, in toto, of course, to another room of the house. The chapel, perhaps, or the library? Sir Harry was horrified at the thought. The first Sir Edward had built that room and installed that panel, and there it would remain!

Lady Marie had sighed, shaken her head at such foolishness, then agreed to group her pieces closer together.

Louisa was dismayed that they would not have no less than three Cleopatras staring down at them. The Hall, with its high, beautiful windows and huge old fireplace, was a family gathering-place. Cleopatra did not add in the least to its comfort. Louisa considered this problem long and hard, but was forced to admit that there was no other room in the house that could even begin to endure the presence of the hangings. In any place else they would be disastrous. Her private opinion, shared by Sir Harry, was that the large oak chest on the stair landing was the very place for them to rest, neatly folded, and out of sight.

Lady Marie, always punctilious in matters of etiquette, did see fit to send Lady Howorthy a cordial little note, telling her of her pleasure in receiving the tapestry, her small efforts to repair it, the place of honor it now took in her family's home. There was no mention of the previous unpleasantness of some eighteen years' duration. Louisa could imagine Lady Howorthy's confusion upon receiving it, a confusion reflected in her somewhat muddled reply.

That a reconciliation was somehow effected she knew. Quite how it came about, she didn't know. Over later years she managed to piece together certain information of the forces that had been at work in the Howorthy household.

To begin with, Aunt Enderbie had severely squelched Lady Howorthy. One thing John did remember was appealing to her for help. Lady Howorthy lived in terror of her husband's aunt and John assured his friends that it took very little effort on her part to have an effect on his mother. Threats of social ostracism were leveled, ridicule piled on her, and inducements of money added, and Lady Howorthy was forced to realize that it was very much to her advantage to ignore the main interest and concern of the last eighteen years of her life, in fact to forget that there had even been a quarrel.

The reconciliation certainly made life easier for the families and all their neighbors. To have the two principal families of one's part of the world not on speaking terms was very awkward indeed. For a time Lady Bardoff had refused to receive anyone who had called on the Howorthys and Lady Howorthy had countered with a similar tactic against the Bardoffs' guests. The intercession of the rector's wife had put an end to this. This wise woman, who knew her husband's parishioners well, had visited the other ladies of the district, brought them to a consensus that there was no reason to withdraw into enemy camps, at least none that they could detect, and then encouraged them to visit *both* households as if nothing curious had happened. She herself set an example by speaking to both ladies at church one Sunday morning, then visiting them the next day, in the opposite order.

Thus, Lady Howorthy had been honored with the first greeting after the service, but Lady Bardoff had had the first visit. When faced with the fact that no one was paying the least attention to their dictums, they had quietly withdrawn them.

It had still been awkward. After all, one could not invite them both to the same party or social gathering. There was one enterprising and sociable lady who solved this quite neatly. She would have two parties in the same week, identical in every last detail, from the food served to the guests invited and how they were entertained, except that Lady Howorthy was invited to one and Lady Bardoff to the other. Among the hostess's friends it was understood that the two parties were to count as but one when the time to reciprocate arose.

Sir Harry's hunting pack had certainly influenced the outcome in favor of reconciliation. He had the finest dogs in the county, the ones with the keenest sense of smell and the greatest determination. Foxes, hares, all small game stood not the slightest chance when Sir Harry's pack was sniffing them out. But the Bardoff estates were small and he could only exercise them over a limited acreage, even with the land around the Colville's hunting box added.

Lord Howorthy, on the other hand, had had singularly ill luck with his kennels. His bitches died in whelping, his best leaders fell into traps and suffered permanent injury, and simply finding enough dogs to take out was a problem at times. But Lord Howorthy was an avid huntsman with the finest game preserves in the area. He had mourned over his kennels for some years, never giving up the effort, until finally he was forced to take up shooting with a sigh. Taking aim at birds was poor sport when compared to sitting a horse and riding hell for leather over the countryside, with frequent stops at the country inns for refreshment along the way. Lady Bardoff's note coupled with the disappearance of a piece of sewing he had never liked in any case, was a godsend. He added his own arguments to those of his aunt and son as they forced the hapless Lady Howorthy to accept peace. Now Lord Howorthy and Sir Harry could look forward to a fine hunting season, roaming over the whole countryside as they galloped after a pack of fine dogs and their quarry.

The most important factor was a very personal one to Lady Howorthy. She, the daughter of a respectable but untitled landowner who had chanced to make a fortune in trade on the side, had received a note offering reconciliation from Lady Bardoff, the daughter of an earl. In her own mind it was Lady Bardoff who made the first gesture of peace. Never mind John and his silly story of that hideous wall hanging. No one in their right mind could want such a thing to the extent of quarreling over it for some eighteen years without even asking for it. If Lady Howorthy had known that her neighbor had wanted it, she would have been glad to get it off her hands and send it over to the Hall. Who would want to have Cleopatra, dressed in some strange costume that was most unfashionable, continually tumbling out of a rug before their very eyes? No, Lady Bardoff had relented for some other reason and that was all that counted to Lady Howorthy. *She* had not backed down. At the insistence of her husband and his aunt she would be condescending, even gracious, in the matter. Not a word of criticism for Lady Bardoff's past behavior would cross her lips, not one. She would act as if the past eighteen years had never been, and take up the threads of a cordial relationship such as neighbors ought to have. And if Lord Howorthy could enjoy his hunting season, so much the better. It would certainly put him in a better frame of mind and make him easier to live with.

John Howorthy was a frequent visitor then. After all, although his love was still far away in London and unapproachable until her mother was by her side to countenance the friendship, he could console himself with long discussions of her beauty, charm and talent with her best friend. Louisa patiently listened to the artless little poems and notes that John was writing for his love, his plans for their future together, his hopes for her speedy return to the Bardoff household. Unwittingly, they were giving Sir Harry some concern and Lord Howorthy much satisfaction. John's father had already heard of his son's strange quest for an end to the feud, Aunt Enderbie having taken him into her confidence. He noted that Tommy was still absent, whether from lack of ardor or from his mother's insistence he didn't know. He thought that a match between his heir and Louisa would be an excellent thing. He had always had a secret liking for the girl. John had chosen well. With his newfound faith in miracles, Lord Howorthy was sure that it would somehow all work out.

Sir Harry was also sure that it would work out, but in a different way. He had observed Louisa's lack of spirits and thought that he knew her well enough to divine at least some of the reason for this. Certainly the presence of her lover should have had the opposite effect on her, he reassured himself. He had an entirely different outcome in mind and John Howorthy's apparent attentions to his daughter were an added complication and not at all agreeable. For once he regretted, briefly, that the feud had ended.

Louisa frequently plagued John with questions about the return of the tapestry. Beyond saying that he had felt that there was someone leaning over his shoulder, just one step behind him, the whole of his journey from London, he could not account for his success. He merely commented that the feeling that he had a guardian angel supporting him had added much to his self confidence and had helped him carry off his difficult role with panache.

XV

After her anger had died down, Louisa thought of her encounter with Lord Geffrey with mortification. The full ramifications of her actions had suddenly struck her! In her efforts to avoid implicating Susan in the affair, she had taken her friend's place. The intrigue, the exchange of notes, the hurried conversations with John, all, all made it seem that she was in love with him, not Susan. And her crowning folly had been that secret note to John. Why couldn't she have sent it to Tommy? She could have relied on him to get the information to his friend. What Lord Geffrey thought of her had been obvious from the expression on his face and the coldness of his manner.

What a figure she had cut! Hissing to him through the open window, begging secrecy, dropping the letter to him. Her behavior was that of a silly, vulgar chit. Engaged to one man, she was entering into a secret correspondence with another, a man of whom her family totally disapproved.

And of all people she could have chosen to expose herself to, Lord Geffrey was the worst. Not that she thought that he would reveal her folly. On the contrary, he was a man of honor who had given his word, a man who would find her conduct particularly repellent for that reason. She had involved him in her intrigue and he was bound to resent that. His niceness of manners, his feeling for what was proper, his basic decency, all would be outraged.

It was cold comfort to her to discover that she cared for his opinion, cared very much indeed. Somehow her feelings had developed beyond the proper regard due to a gentleman of his rank and fortune. She had every reason to feel respect for him: his person was handsome, his manners open and easy, his kindness and friendliness flattering indeed. She was shocked by the sudden realization that this regard had grown into something far stronger. It was an attachment that wreaked far greater havoc with her emotional tranquility than her modest affection for Tommy Colville had ever done. The turmoil of her mind, the sudden breathlessness at the merest thought of him, her desire to hear his name spoken, even the secret smile that came to her lips, all spoke of love.

How could she tell him the truth of the situation that she had dragged him into? It was hardly fitting that she seek him out. Polite young ladies did not do such things. Write a letter? That would be to embark on yet another clandestine correspondence! It was hardly the way to present herself to him to advantage, no matter how noble a tale she told.

True, he would soon learn at least part of the tale, now that John was free to openly court his beloved Ssuan. That Lady Bardoff's approval was necessary for the enterprise would be apparent to all, Mrs. Lauderdale following her friend's lead in everything. She could but pray that Lord Geffrey would recognise this and acquit her of selfish motives for embarking on her course of deceit.

But what use was it to clear her reputation in his eyes, even partially? Louisa had no illusions about her own appeal to the heart of a man like Lord Geffrey. With his handsome person, respected title, and considerable wealth, he could choose any woman of rank for his wife. Certainly a wife of beauty and elegance would be his first choice, the daughter of some aristocratic family. Even innocent Louisa was aware of his reputation for high standards of beauty among the ladies who had passed under his protection. Such a lady as he would choose to marry would be a suitable hostess, serve admirably as the mistress of his many households, and bear him children he could be proud of. The offspring of a mere baronet, albeit one of ancient family and highest respectability, was far beneath his touch. Any love that Louisa felt for him would never be returned.

She thought long and hard about her future. Unrequited love was a most unhappy state of feeling to look forward to. Louisa was a sensible girl, realizing that a lifetime of spinsterhood, spent under the same roof with her mother or perhaps in her brother Ruston's household once he was married, would not suit her in the least. She wanted a life of her own, raising her own family and ordering her own household. It was something she would do well and in which she would find fulfillment. Playing second fiddle in someone else's home would be a barren life indeed.

Marriage to Tommy seemed to be the likeliest solution. She had argued herself back to accepting the status quo! After all, such a course was expected of her. She had previously had every hope of a successful, happy marriage; with discipline and hard work she could still achieve it. Tommy would never know the difference.

Or would he?

Louisa stopped in her tracks, all her planning cast aside. There had always been an understanding between them, albeit an unspoken one, that their affection would deepen into love. Years of working together and living together would only strengthen their affection and liking for one another into something more enduring. Now Louisa knew in her own heart that this was impossible.

Surely Tommy deserved something more. Louisa had been so selfishly involved with her own woe that she had forgotten the happiness of those around her. Tommy ought to have a wife who could love him and only him, as a wife should. His simple, uncomplicated nature could be happy no other way. To enter into a marriage with her heart free was one thing, to marry Tommy with her desperate love for another man, was something else again.

There was nothing to do but break the engagement, unofficial as it was. She would have to approach her father to tell him of her decision, praying that he would forgive her and offer her his help and advice.

Sir Harry proved to be easily approachable. For a man who had expected for some ten years that his daughter would marry a neighbor's son and heir, he was surprisingly sympathetic and unflustered by the change of plans.

Louisa found him in the long gallery, among the portraits of his ancestors. Having a nice sense of family history, he frequently visited there, seeking inspiration from the past baronets and their ladies when faced with a knotty problem.

Louisa, bundled into an ill-fitting morning dress, approached him hesitantly.

"Papa?"

"What? What?" Sir Harry, deep in a reverie before the portrait of his great-grandmother, the lady who had planned the rose garden, looked about him with a scowl on his face. His eyes fell on that lady's namesake and for a startled moment he thought that he was seeing a ghost.

"Oh. Lou, dear. Should you be up and about?" he asked a trifle incoherently, still frowning at her.

Louisa was somewhat quelled by this greeting. "Yes, Papa. Dr. Barnes has even said that I may walk in the garden tomorrow if the sun is shining."

"What? Good, good." He continued to stare at her, still puzzling over his problem.

"Papa, there is something important that I must discuss with you," Louisa said a little desperately.

His daughter's distress penetrated his preoccupation and he was suddenly all concern. "Sit down, Lou, here in this window seat." He took her arm and led her to the casement, considering another query on the advisability of her being out of her room, even out of bed. But a careful look at her told him that in fact she looked much stronger, the bloom even showing in her cheeks.

"Well, well, girl, what's the matter?" he asked in a kindly way. "Just tell your poor old papa what it is all about."

Louisa took heart from his tone and tried to explain. "It is about Tommy, Papa."

"Tommy? Do you miss him so much?" he asked her with surprise.

"No, I mean, yes. I mean that it is about our engagement that I am concerned."

"Ah! Didn't think you were moping for him," he said with relief. "Nice young chap, but . . ."

"Yes, yes, Papa," Louisa said hastily. "I am very fond of Tommy. But . . ."

"Yes, 'but'. That's it exactly," Sir Harry agreed sadly.

"He is a fine young man, all that he ought to be," Louisa said thoughtfully, unaware of the nuances the conversation was taking.

"Fine young man," he nodded.

"Honorable, upright, and an excellent friend."

"Excellent friend."

"And he deserves a wife of great merit."

"Great merit," Sir Harry agreed, worried that the trend of the conversation had perhaps swerved. Well, if he was what she really wanted . . .

"He is worthy of a very special girl. Whoever is able to attach his regard is fortunate indeed."

"Fortunate."

"But he deserves someone who can love him with all her heart! Without reservations!"

"Ah! Exactly!" Sir Harry agreed with enthusiasm. Perhaps it was working out as he hoped. He stared hard at her, his expression one of encouragement.

"I fear that I can offer him no more than a

177

most," she hesitated, chosing her words with care, "a most affectionate regard. And respect, too, of course," she added hastily.

"Of course," Sir Harry echoed, looking very pleased.

"And so I feel that I must break the engagement," Louisa finished with a rush of words. She looked at her father with apprehension and some confusion.

Sir Harry was beaming with approval. "Exactly so. I will speak to Lord Colville about it myself."

"Shouldn't I . . . ?"

Sir Harry ignored the interruption. "After all, Colville and I were the ones who planned this. We ought to be able to unplan it. Don't think Tommy's heart is involved in the matter."

"No, I am sure that it is not," Louisa said faintly. She had never dreamed that it would be this easy!

"Quite. Young chap ought to be in the cavalry. Quite mad about it, too. Too young to marry."

"Yes, Papa."

"You run along and tell your mama what we've decided. Don't worry. I'll deal with the Colvilles. And you'll have more time to look around, too. You'll find someone you're better suited to, I am sure." And with the greatest good humor he sent his daughter away.

The sun suddenly broke through a cloud, lighting up the gallery and in particular playing on the portrait of the first Lady Louisa. Sir Harry looked at her with satisfaction. She had been accounted a great beauty in her day, with fine gray eyes, lovely brown hair, slender figure, beautiful skin, and even a dimple in her cheek when she was pleased and smiled. Her experience had taught her to trust her own judgment and sense, and many people deemed this to be arrogance, but Sir Harry had always admired the soundness of her decisions. She had been an excellent wife and mother, ably assisting her husband in his political career and raising six happy, healthy children. Her memory was still cherished in the district, for her generosity had been proverbial.

Sir Harry had always thought that his daughter was rather like her ancestress, a thought he had kept to himself over the years. He suspected that others would laugh at him, but with a little encouragement, he was sure that they too would appreciate the resemblance. He vowed that this time he would see to it that Louisa had a better chance to show to advantage. Sitting happily in the sunlight, he wove his schemes and ambitions for his favorite child.

XVI

Sir Harry lost no time in traveling to London and seeking out Lord Colville for an interview. He approached his old friend with an expression of serious concern, meeting him at Brooke's.

After a suitable conversation on the weather, a pair of bays coming up for sale, and the quality of the wine they had been served, Sir Harry broached the subject of the engagement rather bluntly.

"It's about Tommy and Lou, Colly," he said bruskly.

"Oh?" Lord Colville said cautiously. He had an uneasy feeling that he saw the direction the conversation would take.

"The engagement."

"Oh." An expression of gloom covered his face as he observed Sir Harry's serious expression.

"Louisa and I feel that the young couple's affections aren't seriously engaged." Sir Harry had considered his words carefully in advance and was quite proud of them.

"Never said it was a love match," grumbled Tommy's father.

"Quite, quite," Sir Harry said soothingly. "Lou ain't looking for romance. She is a good, sensible girl and knows better. We just want to make sure that they could be happy together, Colly. Really happy."

"Oh." The gloom deepened.

"Childhood friendship all well and good," Sir Harry said elliptically.

"But not enough?" Lord Colville prompted sadly.

"Exactly." Sir Harry said with satisfaction, pleased that his point had been made for him.

Lord Colville sighed deeply. "Afraid it would come to this. Been too good to last. We've actually had the same chef for six whole months. A Frenchie. Lou used to talk to him some, cheer him up. In French, you know."

Sir Harry was instantly sympathetic. "The truffle soup?"

Lord Colville nodded affirmatively.

"The braised duck?" Sir Harry pressed anxiously. He had had several excellent meals at the Colville table that spring and hated to contemplate their end.

"The braised duck," Lord Colville confirmed. "And he has a damned nice way with fish." He sighed deeply. "I was hoping to get him down to the country. Pity to waste him."

"Perhaps Louisa can visit. After all, we don't want to end the friendship. Just the engagement."

Lord Colville perked up. "Visit. Good thought, Harry. Will scotch any rumors of a fight, too."

Sir Harry, who had not considered this detail before, agreed vigorously. "No reason why she can't drop by often. You're right about the chef. Pity to waste him. Now all we have to do is tell Tommy."

"Won't bother him a bit, I fear."

"And place an announcement in the *Times* withdrawing the engagement." Sir Harry ended with satisfaction.

"Eh? Can't do that, old boy!" Lord Colville protested vigorously.

"What? What? Why not?" Sir Harry sputtered.

"Never announced it in the first place."

Sir Harry looked at his friend in dismay, much struck with the truth of the comment.

"But everyone knows about it. Expect it. Even have a bet on it in the book right here. May or June. Have to tell them it's off somehow? Wouldn't be right not to."

Lord Colville mulled over this problem, then shrugged his shoulders.

"Well, we'll deal with that later. Have to tell Tommy about it first."

"Right. First things first."

"But what am I going to do with the boy?" Lord Colville asked with dismay. "I've been relying on having Louisa take a hand with him. Settle him down, you know."

Sir Harry seized his opportunity for putting in a word for the young man. "Cavalry."

"Cavalry? His mother don't like the notion. She says it's just a passing fancy."

Sir Harry shook his head vigorously to disabuse his friend of that theory. "Cavalry's the thing. Lady Colville, God bless her, is just being protective. Any mother would. But Tommy's past that now," he said reassuringly. "He's old enough to start taking care of himself. High time."

"Cavalry!" Lord Colville appeared to like the sound of the word. And on this note the two men set out in search of the ex-fiancé.

They ran him to ground in his father's stables, glumly examining the hoof of his favorite mount. His father and Sir Harry persuaded him to leave off prying for the stone in the hoof and hurried him into the house. The head groom could see to the animal's comfort.

Once they had reached the privacy of the library, Lord Colville laid a fatherly arm around the young man's shoulders and broke the news as gently as he knew how.

184

"Afraid the engagement is off, Tommy," he said sadly.

"Off? Louisa's crying off?" Tommy asked with surprised interest.

Sir Harry, perceiving that more explanation was due, if not necessary, entered the breach. "She's still dashed fond of you, Tommy. But her glimpse of the world makes her feel that a stronger attachment is needed to make a happy marriage."

Tommy agreed enthusiastically. "The very thing," he agreed. He too had realized that there were couples, such as John and Susan, whose feelings ran deeper than his for Louisa. Besides, he was still smarting from his visit to his grandmother. The prospect of a lifetime of heeding Louisa's urgings had filled him with some dismay. She was a real brick of a girl, but he thought that he wanted something more restful in a wife.

Lord Colville, glad that his son was taking the news with such understanding, thumped him on the back. "I'm buying you a commission, Tommy. You'll need something to keep you busy now that you aren't getting married. That is, if you still want to join up with the cavalry. A hussar regiment, perhaps?"

For a moment there was a stunned silence.

"The cavalry!" Tommy shouted with joy. He was dizzy with the very thought of it. A happy picture of horses and uniforms and formations and messmates passed before his eyes, then one of charges and battles and glory. Everything he had ever dreamed of was suddenly being offered to him without his even asking.

He was sobered by the thought of how much he owed Louisa. He knew that she had been aware of his burning ambition and he was certain that this was what had motivated her to withdraw from the engagement, something that *he* in all honor, could not have done. She was clearing the way for his happiness. And at what a sacrifice! That marriage was the goal of all young women he knew. But Louisa had bravely overturned their parents' plans, and her own future, to free him. What a great friend she was! A real brick of a girl.

"Sir, it's what I want above all else. It is very noble of Louisa to withdraw her claims and allow me to pursue it," he said earnestly.

Lord Colville wasn't listening. "Your mother won't like it a bit, but that can't be helped. She'll get over it. I'll explain to her how important it is to you."

Tommy said gratefully. "Thank you, sir." It was a relief to have this unpleasant task, one that he hadn't even thought of, taken from his hands.

"Sir Harry says that Louisa can visit often."

"Mama will like that."

"And talk French to André."

"Gaston."

"No need for her to stand on ceremony."

Tommy was struck with a noble thought. "Sir

Harry, I am deeply appreciative of what Louisa has done for me."

"You can thank her yourself, lad, next time you see her. You might just pop down to the country for a visit," he added dryly. "You would be more than welcome."

"Once I am settled in my career, it won't take me but a few years, I imagine . . ."

"If that, my boy, if that," Sir Harry said generously.

"And if Louisa will consider me, and if she is still unattached, I would be honored to make her my wife," he ended nobly, squelching all thoughts of that dreadful interview with the dowager.

Sir Harry looked at him with surprise. "What? What?" he asked anxiously.

Lord Colville cheered up. "Good thought, Tommy! Give the two of you a chance to get your feet on the ground, get some experience under your belt. Then you can make a match of it. Eh, Sir Harry?"

Sir Harry frowned. This was *not* what he had had in mind. "Good of you to offer, Tommy. Appreciate it," he said doubtfully.

"Although I know that a girl like Louisa will be snapped up quickly, in all likelihood," young Colville added hastily.

Sir Harry smiled, able to relax with this thought. "Exactly. She will find some upstanding man and make a match of it! No need for you to worry!"

187

Tommy continued to be noble. "But if not . . . If no one has won her heart . . . Well, if not then I will certainly offer for her. She's a great girl!"

"Great girl," Sir Harry agreed unhappily.

"Won't ever come to that," Lord Colville said mournfully. "Not a chance. Pity. I'm quite attached to her, you know. We all are, I dare say. Well, I'll be able to go back to Hampshire, now."

He then ordered a bottle brought up from the cellar. When it appeared, the three men uncorked it and solemnly sampled it, toasting Louisa and Tommy's future, but separate happiness. Ross, the butler, caught the gist of these proceedings and was duly confused and shocked by them, but at least the forewärning allowed him to spread the word among his minions and prepare for the crisis that would soon be upon them when Lady Colville heard that her son was due to join a hussar regiment, and when the chef heard that Miss Louisa would not become a member of the household.

Later that evening, Sir Harry was struck with inspiration. Fetching Lord Colville, still somewhat dazed after a session with his wife, he headed for Brooke's. Its rooms were crowded with men when they arrived and they bowed to many acquaintances. He lead Lord Colville into the inner sanctum.

The betting book at Brooke's recorded many eccentric wagers. There were races of all sorts listed, even one between two flies, and two men had gone so far as to lay wagers on the longevity of certain of their contemporaries. Sir Harry flipped through the pages, ignoring the grumbling of his companion.

He quickly found what he wanted. Lady Bardoff had been up in arms when she had heard that a Mr. T and a Sir J had laid down a pony each against *when,* not if, her daughter would marry Tommy Colville, this before there had been any sort of announcement. To have her daughter's name bandied about in such a way was mortifying. Sir Harry thought it harmless enough and had placated her in an off-handed way, simply shrugging off her demands for action. When friends laughingly pointed out the entry to him, he had inspected it carefully, then seized the first opportunity to assure his spouse that it was innocuous indeed, especially when compared to some of the others.

With much satisfaction, he called for a quill and some ink, reassuring Lord Colville that this was the very thing. By the time the writing material had arrived, a small crowd of members had gathered about them, expectant of some new amusement.

Sir Harry grabbed the pen and leaned over the book, spectacles in place. With a flourish he ran the line through the entry.

"I thought of droppin' a word into Sally Jersey's ear, Colly," he explained to his still baffled friend confidentially. "It would have been all over Town in no time. But then this seemed even better."

He returned the pen and ink to the startled

waiter, and with a bow prepared to take leave of his audience. A young dandy pushed his way forward to see the book and what had been done to it.

"Dash it all, Sir Harry. What's the meaning of this? Has a different month been chosen? I say, tell us what it's all about."

Sir Harry turned to his questioner with every appearance of good humor. "Month? Month for what?"

"Why, for the wedding, of course."

"Wedding?"

"Between your daughter and Lord Colville's son," the young man said with asperity.

"Wedding? How can there be a wedding? Have we announced an engagement, Colly?"

Lord Colville considered this seriously. "No. No engagement," he replied.

"Can't get married without an engagement," Sir Harry explained kindly.

"No engagement?" someone said in a shocked voice.

"Heavens, no," Sir Harry said cheerfully.

"Can't. Tommy's joining the hussars. Wouldn't do to get married *and* take up a cornetcy," Lord Colville explained.

And with that, the fathers sauntered out, arm in arm, leaving a startled company behind them.

XVII

The ladies were very busy over the next few weeks. Louisa for one was refurbishing her wardrobe in toto. There were many letters and parcels being sent between the Hall and the fashionable London modistes as she set about her task.

Despite the lateness of the Season, Sir Harry had insisted that Louisa purchase many new dresses to fit her new figure. Lady Bardoff had tried to insist that her daughter was still unwell and that she would soon regain her former plumpness. Dr. Barnes, who had cared for the family for many years, disagreed. He insisted that Louisa was wonderfully recuperated, although still in need of exercise to regain her tone. He held that her present abhorrence of cream puffs, pastries and sweets was a vast improvement, that Lady Bardoff should not encourage her to join her mother in partaking of them, that a diet of plainly dressed meat and vegetables was a healthy one, even better if augmented by fruits from the cold frames and hothouses.

Lady Bardoff countered with the theories of Sir Q and Dr. M, who both held that true health could only be found in the full-bodied person. Louisa was certainly *not* full-bodied. Lady Bardoff went on to hold herself up as an example of the rightness of the theory. Dr. Barnes and Sir Harry, who had suffered through innumerable colds, palpitations of the heart, and spells of faintness, looked doubtful. Sir Harry had ended the matter by saying heartily that Louisa should be allowed to eat whatever she wanted to eat and if it kept her thin, then she would need to get some new clothes.

With that the refurbishing began. Whole bolts of material, yards of lace, swatches of fabrics, patterns of embroidery, samples of trimmings, all flowed between London and the country. Louisa revelled in yards of delicate muslin, luxurious silk, cambric, poplin and other fabrics. At her father's insistence, poor Lady Bardoff took little hand in the matter. Exhausted from her hours of nursing her daughter, she was allowed to rest, leaving the decisions to Louisa. Sir Harry was most solicitous of his wife's health, even carrying her off to rest near her torn up gardens whenever it came time to write the letters giving the final orders for one of Louisa's gowns. He held that Louisa needed an interest to refresh her mind, and that her wardrobe was the very thing. Lady Bardoff, overwhelmed with her husband's sudden devotion, could only agree. And for the first time, Louisa's walking dresses, riding habits, evening gowns, shawls, bonnets, boots, pelisses, even her parasols, were truly hers.

At the London end of the process were the countess and Susan, co-ordinating the activities of the various dressmakers. Lady Bardoff's mother had thrown herself wholeheartedly into the scheme, bustling from shop to shop, matching colors, entering into long discussions with modistes, and spending a great deal of money. She wrote solicitous letters to her daughter to accompany every parcel of gowns and materials, letters full of worry and concern that Lady Marie had ruined her own health, was allowing herself too little time to rest, was not eating properly, was taking too much responsibility into her own hands. The countess even went so far as to encourage her daughter's predilection for gardening, if it would divert her attention from the rapidly building wardrobe.

Louisa's measurements had been taken most carefully, her mother moaning over her thinness all the while, then sent to London. The most expensive modiste on Bond Street assured the countess that they would be sufficient. If necessary, she would even scour the city for a girl of the exact dimensions to stand in for the fittings. The size of the orders so late in the Season made it well worth her while. Sir Harry had ordered that no expense be spared and his mother-in-law had decided to pay some of the bills herself in order to see that her granddaughter was properly turned out. Both were already concocting schemes for presenting the new Louisa to Society, despite the scarcity of company in Town. With the help of the local dressmaker, who saw to whatever slight alterations were needed, their money was well spent.

Louisa's closets were soon filled with beautiful clothes. Ballgowns of silk and satin and sarsonet, evening gowns of crepe and jaconet muslin, a taffeta opera cloak trimmed with velvet, morning half-dresses of figured muslin and Berlin silk, carriage dresses of cambric, walking dresses, afternoon dresses, Norwich shawls, silver-net drapery, shoes, halfboots, slippers, reticules, gloves, stockings, all arrived in parcel after parcel. The styles were simple, the colors less insipid than what she had previously worn, and all contrived to make Louisa look radiant. The profusion even enabled her to forget for a few brief moments her unhappy state of mind, and at other times it gave her hope that perhaps she might yet win Lord Geffrey's heart.

She would have been surprised at the amount of comment her activities, and those by others for her, were stimulating. Two ladies in particular had observed her closely and frequently exchanged views with one another on the subject.

"She's but a dab of a girl, mind you," Mrs. Enderbie grumbled. "Good eyes and skin, lovely hair, and pretty enough manners, not the least bit high in the instep, nor is she missish, but her figure is far too plump. I finally had to take a look at her myself, you know. I rarely go abroad these days but it seemed to me that any young lady who could attach the devotion of no less than three young men ought to be inspected in person."

"Three?" Lady Geffrey said doubtfully.

"Three. I hear that Tommy Colville wants to marry her after he has established his career in the hussars," Mrs. Enderbie said with only a hint of sarcasm in her voice. She was gratified by the expression of surprise that this piece of news drew from her guest. She continued.

"I attended that ball in her honor for that very purpose. What a disappointment! The dowdiest gown possible! Most inappropriate. All those flounces and ruffles puffed her out even more! But the young men didn't seem to mind. They were buzzing around her like bees to honey and I dare say that they all seemed to enjoy her company. Even that clumsy Freddy Whipple was showing to advantage with her."

"Perhaps she puts them at ease."

"That is all well and good, my dear, but in my day real beauty counted for something. Why, I remember . . ." Mrs. Enderbie continued for some time with her reminiscences, while Lady Geffrey's thoughts ranged elsewhere.

"She was named after a previous Lady Bardoff, wasn't she?" interrupted Lady Geffrey. "One who was quite a beauty in her day, I understand."

"The first Louisa?" Mrs. Enderbie asked with surprise. "She was *the* beauty of her day. I remember meeting her when I was quite young, you know. Even in her old age she had an air about her. Fine eyes, elegant hands, marvelous skin. People still told tales of her conquests, but she was said to have lived quite happily with her husband after their marriage, raising a large family. She spent most of her time in the country or working with her husband in his political career, and was said to be contented with her married life."

"Perhaps her namesake takes after her in some ways," Lady Geffrey murmured.

Mrs. Enderbie snorted and began to protest, then cut her comments off. She stared at her friend in dismay, but thought hard, understanding her motive for this piece of wishful thinking. Besides, the dresses had been all wrong, wrong cut, wrong color, but perhaps . . . .

"I suppose that something could be done with her," she allowed generously, letting the overplumpness slip by.

"I hope that it is being done now," Lady Geffrey said bluntly. The thought of her only child making a fool of himself over some silly country miss with no pretensions to style and elegance, much less beauty, was more than her pride could bear. Francis deserved the best, and she prayed that if he really did care for this girl, that Louisa would be made more presentable. Whatever had possessed Francis to throw his cap over the windmill for such a plain girl, even one with a reputation for kindness and amusing conversation, was beyond the scope of her imagination.

"Her grandmother is making a great bustle in the shops, despite the lateness of the Season. Mme. Dupré hinted but yesterday that the gowns being made for the young lady are among the most ravishing she has ever seen," Mirs. Enderbie added kindly.

"Why make her a new wardrobe at all?" Lady Geffrey asked thoughtfully. "Although she certainly needed one, I can't imagine her mother admitting to it. After all, the old gowns were all of Lady Marie's choosing!"

"Haven't you heard? She has grown most distressingly thin! Her mother is quite beside herself."

Lady Geffrey sighed. From a plump pigeon to a skinny scarecrow. What had Francis come to?

She brightened at a new thought. "Perhaps she will settle for John Howorthy!" she said hopefully. "The families have suddenly made peace with one another after all these years. It would seem to point in that direction."

Mrs. Enderbie struggled with her conscience, then settled for a compromise. "Rather, the mothers have ended their foolishness!" she said tartly. Family pride forbade her from divulging the silly tale that John had told her. That two women could quarrel bitterly for so many years over a mere wall-hanging, and an ugly one at that, was beyond the bounds of reason. She considered the suggestion carefully and added, "He was extremely anxious to bring the families together, that is certain. He was making a cake of himself trying to find the reason for the ill will between the ladies."

"And what was the cause of it all?" Lady Geffrey asked innocently. "It must have something monstrous to create such strong feeling all these years."

Mrs. Enderbie winced. "Monstrous would be one way to describe it," she agreed without thinking. Then realizing that she had said too much, she quickly shut the door on any further confidences. "But I fear that even John is unsure of their exact nature. Somehow Louisa ferreted it out and took steps to deal with the breach."

"Then Louisa must be as interested in John as he is in her!" Lady Geffrey said happily, diverted from the tempting tidbit of gossip she had been fishing for. "There can be no other reason for her to pursue a solution so eagerly!" The thought that her son's role had grown to exaggerated proportions in her own mind and could be reasonably trimmed back pleased her.

Mrs. Enderbie looked at her contemptuously. She had not raised Francis Geffrey's name, but had included it in all of her calculations, assuming that her friend was doing likewise. That Lady Geffrey was anxious over her son's future she could appreciate. He would need to marry and establish a nursery if the family's name and title were to continue in the direct male line. But she felt that Lady Geffrey was failing to appreciate the niceness of his attentions to Miss Bardoff. She threw out a delicate line of her own.

"Young Howorthy was certainly attentative enough when Miss Bardoff fell ill. He helped to assist her from the ballroom," she said casually.

Lady Geffrey resolutely refused to take the bait. "Exactly! Young Colville was nowhere to be found. If it hadn't been for Mr. Howorthy and Mr. Whipple, Louisa would have been in sad straits indeed."

"Mr. Whipple? He surely gave her his arm in the ballroom, but I recollect that an other escorted her from it."

"In any case," Lady Geffrey said hurriedly, "John Howorthy was beside her throughout, except to explain the case to Tommy Colville and his parents. A most particular sign of attachment, I would say!"

"Most particular," agreed Mrs. Enderbie dryly.

"I think that I shall make it a point to visit the

Countess of Sitwell tomorrow. Just to see how things are with her."

"You must tell me what you hear." And with this agreed to, the ladies' conversation ranged over other fields.

XVIII

————————

It was fortunate for Lady Geffrey's peace of mind that only her son knew how foolish he had been. His mother would have been shocked and bewildered by his wild chase into the countryside, and she would have been baffled by the reason for it. Why bother to take such extreme measures to help a girl he had no responsibility for, in fact a girl whom he considered to be lacking in all propriety and decorum. Fustian! A sane man did not do such things.

Lord Geffrey had finally begun to face his motives for his escapades. He supposed that strictly speaking, he was *not* a sane man. At the age of thirty, with much worldly experience behind him and a fastidious taste in women fully developed, he had fallen in love with a girl in her teens. She had little to recommend her, no great fortune, no grand family alliance to offer, no stunning beauty, and furthermore, she was engaged to one man and intriguing with another. He had refused to acknowledge that his attachment was deeper than that formed by mild amusement at the cleverness and originality of the young lady in question. That she was kindhearted in most of her dealings with people he also appreciated. But even if there had been no engagement to Tommy Colville and no flirtation with John Howorthy, she would have been eminently unsuitable!

And yet Lord Geffrey had galloped after her supposed seducer to rescue her from a foolhardy elopement. He had stepped back into her life repeatedly, despite assurances to himself that he had washed his hands of her. He had even made one of her young men his protegé, introducing him into the world of horses. Attending the ball in her honor had been the supreme folly! Once there, despite all efforts on his part to avoid her, she had collapsed in his arms, violently ill. He had followed this up with a visit to her in the country and found himself enmeshed in intrigue, the carrier of a sordid, clandestine love note.

Here Lord Geffrey pulled himself up sharply. Was he sure that that was truly the case? It *had* been clandestine, but he had attributed to it a degree of intrigue and romance that would have been found only between the covers of a popular novel. In all honesty, the outcome of that note was not what he had expected. True, John Howorthy had behaved in a most peculiar fashion, muttering something about Cleopatra's carpet and dashing off to the country to snatch just such a rug from his parents' house to deliver to the Bardoffs'. Damn that scrap of material, that rag! It just didn't make sense, especially now that the Bardoffs and the Howorthys were back on a friendly footing. How did this carpet fit into the picture? In hard terms, the results of that so-called love note was to end an embarrassing and long-standing feud between two respectable families, and somehow the rug had fit in.

And then Louisa had broken the engagement. Scropes, damn his eyes, had been at Brooke's that evening the two fathers had made their flamboyant gesture, and he had hurried to find Lord Geffrey, anxious to be the first to tell him the news. Geffrey winced as he recalled the tone of the conversation, the arch raillery with which Scropes had offered his 'sincerest' congratulations on having his way made clear to marry Louisa. It had taken all of his hauteur and self control to mount a counterattack of such devastating effect that Scropes had slunk off, too browbeaten with ridicule to even consider sharing his amusing tale with the Town.

After that Lord Geffrey had gone into seculsion,

moping about his town house and ignoring all invitations. A fast gallop in the early morning mists of Hyde Park was his only excursion, and this was not enough to protect him from the thundering scolds delivered by Lady Geffrey, who accused him of sulking most childishly and demanded to know the reason for it.

On one of these dawn excursions he encountered another player in the drama. Tommy Colville was out on a big roan stallion, trying the horse's paces with delight. He was happily preparing for his entry into the hussars as a cornet, even going to the extent of selling his team and purchasing this roan and two other hacks suitable for military service. Upon perceiving a friend, Tommy hallooed him and galloped over for a talk.

"Lord Geffrey, the very person I've been wanting to see!" he exclaimed.

"I'm awed by your interest," Lord Geffrey answered with amusement, his good humor returning with this meeting with a young man he truly liked. "I hear that you are to enter the hussars. I congratulate you!"

Although temporarily abashed by the greeting he had received, Tommy's spirits soared at the mention of the hussars. "It is precisely that which I wanted to tell you about! Is it not the greatest thing?" And he rattled on for some minutes giving his mentor the details of his regiment, where he would be stationed, and which of his acquaintances he expected to encounter.

"I apprehend that that this roan will go with you?" Lord Geffrey asked when the spate of words had finally dwindled.

This brought on an even more excited description of horseflesh. The roan's shoulders, posterns, back, hocks, in short, every part of its anatomy, were discussed and analyzed. This led to the team of horses he had sold, who had bought them, what fine horseflesh they were. Tommy found it a most satisfying conversation.

Even Tommy eventually ran out of things to say about horses and the two men found themselves moving side by side down the path, their mounts at an amiable walk.

"It's the damnedest thing how everything has worked out so well, sir," he suddenly confided.

"You are fortunate to be entering on a career that suits you so well," Lord Geffrey said kindly.

"It's even more than that! You've heard, haven't you, that Louisa's mama and Lady Howorthy have made their peace? I don't know how it came about, but it's the greatest thing!"

"It is indeed wonderful that such a long-standing quarrel has come to an end."

"Yes. And it leaves the way open for John, you know," Tommy said naively.

Lord Geffrey stiffened, then was forced to attend

to his high-strung mount, which had taken exception to a sudden tightening of the reins.

"I am sure that this pleases Miss Bardoff," he said dryly, anger rising in him.

"She's as merry as a gig about it," Tommy acknowledged cheerfully. "So are Sir Harry and Lord Howorthy. The two gentlemen are already planning the next Hunt, no matter that it's months off."

They were approaching a gate to the park and Lord Geffrey saw it as a means to escape. With a polite word of good luck to the new young officer, he made his way back to his own house.

He was much subdued for the next several days. Despite the ache in his heart, he wanted Louisa to have every chance in the world for happiness and if she loved John Howorthy, so be it. For a time he toyed with the idea of taking himself away, traveling abroad in the hope that he would be able to forget her. Instead, the certainty grew within him that he wanted to still be able to see her even if only as a friend. Furthermore, his conscience told him that he owed her an apology for the bad opinion he had so impetuously formed of her. He had either painted her to be a saint or a devil, depending on his current whim, forgetting all logic and common sense. He had missed the fact that she was very much a human being. He was sure that the coldness of his manner during their last conversation had been noticed by her, and he fancied that her feelings had been hurt by it. He must swallow his pride and make overtures to renew the friendship. Or at the very least he must make his apologies.

Necessary business on his own property made it possible to pass within a few miles of Bardoff Hall a day or two later, and he forced himself to seize the opportunity. He arrived on horseback to find the doors of the Hall flung open to the unseasonably gentle breezes. Sir Harry, followed by several hounds, was walking in the park and greeted his unexpected guest enthusiastically.

"Geffrey, what brings you to this part of the world?" he shouted out, disdaining all ceremony.

Lord Geffrey dismounted and approached his host. Now that the die was cast, he felt relaxed and cheerful.

"I've been called to one of my estates, and since it lies beyond here I could not help but stop to see how things are with you and your family."

"Things are capital! Capital! I can finally speak to Howorthy after all these years and we are making plans for next winter. We've many improvements in mind, I assure you!" As they approached the house, Sir Harry expounded at great length on just what was to be done. The dogs yapped cheerfully at his heels, Lord Geffrey's horse, worn by the miles he had covered, ambled comfortably behind his master, and the two men enjoyed their talk.

Sir Harry lead Lord Geffrey to the side of the house. A shout to the stables brought a boy running to take the horse and with a brief explanation that his wife was calling on a friend, he led the way informally through the french windows on the terrace into a charming sitting room.

The room was on a corner of the house and received the southern light and its many windows made it full of the day's brightness. There were pots and pots of plants thriving there, adding their charm to a room that was a trifle shabby but eminently comfortable. Two massive armchairs sat next to a cold grate and looked to be invitingly comfortable.

"This is the best room in the whole place," Sir Harry confided as he led his guest to the chairs. "No design, no one period, no style, just plain comfortable." He paused to tug a bellpull, then settled down with a sigh.

Lord Geffrey murmured his appreciation. The room's homely comforts included a spectacular view of the park and the fields beyond it. Somewhere in the background a church steeple rose, but no other building was in sight to mar the spectacle.

The door opened suddenly and Louisa walked into the room. She was dressed in an old morning gown that had been taken in but still hung a trifle, giving her an odd appearance. "Papa, Winnet says that you have a guest!" she scolded accusingly. The butler entered on her heels, a tray of Sir Harry's favorite sherry and cakes in his hands.

Sir Harry laughed and gave his daughter a kiss. "Sorry, puss. Should I have sent word to you? You're not usually one to stand on ceremony."

Louisa was suddenly aware of Lord Geffrey's presence. To the surprise of the two men, she blushed deeply, her hands flying to her untidy hair and shabby gown. She could not decide what to do first: tuck in her hair or twitch her dress. With a closet full of new clothes she had to be wearing this old rag! Lord Geffrey had never seen her so ill at ease before, and her obvious embarrassment over her appearance was new for her. It slowly dawned on Sir Harry that he should have in fact sent word to her.

She dropped into a slight curtsey and murmured a shy greeting. Sir Harry, apparently unaware of her lack of ease, cheerfully told Winnet to fetch a chair for Miss Lou. Despite her protests, he insisted that she sit down and partake of the refreshments.

Had she but known it, she was looking well indeed. Lord Geffrey was surprised to see that despite her slenderness, she bloomed with health. She had been overseeing the replanting of the garden and the fresh air had added color to her cheeks. And her newfound slimness displayed the finely molded bone structure of her face to advantage. Lord Geffrey found it difficult to keep his eyes off her, or to even attend to his host's conversation. A good natured tease from her father brought a flashing smile to Louisa's face and Lord

Geffrey almost expressed aloud his pleasure that her dimple was as enticing as ever.

Once the young people were more at their ease, Sir Harry turned the conversation to the alterations his lady was making on the grounds. Lord Geffrey replied with polite interest, asking after the quarry he had so haplessly investigated on his last visit.

"Quarry? You wouldn't believe that it had ever been such a thing," Sir Harry laughed.

"Mama has transplanted it wholesale, my lord," Louisa agreed with a chuckle. "She has replanted it with whole trees."

"Have to say one thing for Marie, she has an eye for flowers and shrubs," Sir Harry said expansively.

"And the pool and the waterfall? How do they fare?" Lord Geffrey asked with a smile.

"Flooded, the last big rain," Sir Harry said succinctly. "Nearly ruined the birch trees she had had brought in."

"We have had to install drains and pumps," Louisa added cheerfully. "But all goes well now."

"Let us show it to you!" Sir Harry suddenly offered. Without waiting for the others to reply, he led the way out of the open windows and took the path toward the quarry. Louisa shyly took Lord Geffrey's proffered arm and allowed him to lead her through the window.

XIX

The dogs, which had been waiting patiently on the terrace for their master to reappear, barked cheerfully and frisked about his heels. By the time they had reached the quarry, they were two parties. Sir Harry had forged on ahead, surrounded by the dogs he was struggling to keep in order. They were enraptured by the newly turned earth and had a strong desire to dig up the just planted shrubs. Well behind the turmoil walked Lord Geffrey and Louisa. He tenderly assisted her over the still rough path, carefully moving aside occasional branches that might pull at her dress and hair.

When they reached the quarry, Sir Harry had already circled to the other side.

"Judging from your father's shouts, one of his pointers has gone off after a bird," he remarked easily as they sat down on a small, rustic bench.

Louisa chuckled. "They are always doing so! Mama will be most distressed that he brought the dogs here, they dig about so. And one is forever wandering off into the shrubbery and nothing will do but that Papa wander off after it."

The distant baying of the hounds proved her point. Sir Harry's party was scattered through the woods.

" 'Tis a most pretty view," Lord Geffrey said appreciatively.

Louisa's hands were twisting a ribbon of her gown. "Very pretty," she agreed.

Suddenly faced with the interview he had so long looked forward to, Lord Geffrey found himself at a loss for words, a lowering experience for a man of his address.

"Miss Bardoff . . ."

"Lord Geffrey?"

"Miss Bardoff, I feel that an apology is due you for my conduct when last we met. I was most unforgivably rude to you!"

Louisa blushed. "I had given you good reason to be so. My conduct must have aroused your contempt."

"I don't care about that! It was not my place to judge you. I should never have allowed myself to question the probity of your conduct or the purity of your motives." In his earnestness Lord Geffrey failed to appreciate the pomposity of his statement, and Louisa hid a smile.

"To involve you in a clandestine correspondence, even one embarked upon with the best of motives, was not at all the thing for me to do," Louisa protested.

"I still don't understand what it was all about," Lord Geffrey admitted. "Young Howorthy made some comment about Cleopatra's Carpet that I found quite bewildering! But I can see that the outcome would appear to be peace between your families, and that is all to the good."

Louisa laughed aloud. "Oh, dear! I must show it to you. It is really quite dreadful."

"I would never dream of asking that of you," Lord Geffrey protested. "My sole concern in the matter is that . . . Well, I mean to say that I have the highest regard for you. No matter what has happened . . . I mean, I saw you and Howorthy at the Atwell . . ." Lord Geffrey stopped, floundering, and took hold of himself. "Whatever is the outcome with Howorthy, I want to remain your friend, even if that is all that I can be." He had taken her hand in his own and was holding it tightly.

Louisa looked at him with shocked surprise. He still thought that her interest in John was a personal one! She was at first amused, then touched, that a man of his pride was still proffering friendship, despite his bad opinion of her. Then the hint that he might want more struck her with its full force, stunning her. For a moment she could not breathe as the full impact of his statement made itself felt in her mind. He loved her!

Her heart sang for joy as she finally let herself believe that he loved her, loved her so much that he could not reject her despite her imagined misconduct and her supposed attachment to another man. And he was telling her this as she sat in her oldest, shabbiest gown, with her hair hanging down in wisps!

"I think that we can expect a happy resolution of John's affairs," she said gently.

"Oh?" Lord Geffrey was clearly disappointed and Louisa could not resist teasing him a bit more.

"I believe that even Lady Howorthy will approve!" she added pensively. "Of course, there is no dowry to speak of, but the Howorthy family is quite well off, so that needn't be a major consideration."

"How fortunate," Lord Geffrey said glumly.

"And Lady Howorthy will be quite pleased with the family connection."

"But of course."

"To have her son marry the great-granddaughter of a duke will be most pleasing."

Lord Geffrey frowned. Duke? He recalled no such personage on either side of Louisa's family. There was the earl, of course . . .

"It is a pity that the late Mr. Lauderdale had no title of his own, not even a courtesy one, but it is to be hoped that the Scarwoods will step in and help out in some way. One would expect at least a small reception from them."

"Lauderdale?"

"Yes. Susan has only just met Lady Howorthy; they had dinner for us last night. That is where she and my mama and her mama are today, calling to thank Lady Howorthy for such a lovely evening."

"You mean that John Howorthy is going to marry Susan Lauderdale?" Lord Geffrey asked angrily.

"But of course! He has always been most particular in his attentions to her, when he was able. It was only this silly feud and Mrs. Lauderdale's adherence to Mama's point of view in it that made the subterfuge necessary. We have been trying to sort it out for their sakes for so long now!" She smiled up mischievously at him.

Lord Geffrey sat staring at her for some minutes, trying to assimilate the facts she had given him. In his confusion he had forgotten his high sounding phrases. The one thought that kept forcing itself upon him was that Louisa, his Louisa, was not engaged to Tommy Colville, nor was she in love with John Howorthy. She was entirely free and unattached! For the first time since he had known her she was able to receive his addresses, and for the first time he felt that she might welcome them.

"Miss Bardoff?" he asked suddenly.

"Lord Geffrey?" Louisa glanced up from her

careful inspection of the quarry she already knew very well indeed.

"Will you marry me? I love you most dearly."

"Yes, I will."

"I know that it is very sudden, but if you will agree I will do everything in my power to make you happy."

"I do agree."

"I have loved you for some time now. I just couldn't say anything, what with you being betrothed to Tommy and my damnedest stupidity over the Howorthy thing."

"I love you, too," Louisa said patiently. Surely sooner or later he would hear what she was saying.

"What? You love me? Then you *will* marry me?"

"Of course I will."

"Louisa!" He slipped his arm around her shoulders, used his free hand to tilt her chin up, and kissed her long and thoroughly. She clung to him happily. So this was what sent lovers into the clouds! Eventually he was murmuring into her hair as she snuggled into his arms.

"Good Lord!" he suddenly swore.

"Yes?" she asked anxiously.

"I forgot to ask your father first. I haven't his permission to ask for your hand."

Louisa looked at him with some confusion. Surely her father's subterfuge to get them alone had been obvious? Then she said with a shrug, "You must ask him now, I suppose. He is about some-place." She looked around vaguely.

"I suppose that I could go look for him," her lover offered doubtfully.

The sound of the dogs could be heard some little distance off. It occurred to Louisa that if she let her parent wander at will, she might never get her engagement settled. Releasing herself from Lord Geffrey's arms, she took charge of the situation.

"Eddie! Harry, Charlie! Come boys!" The sound of the barking turned back in their direction. "Papa has named them all after kings and queens, you know. Mama doesn't like it at all, but there you have it! Papa *would* have his way in the matter!"

A crashing sound in the underbrush warned them of the approaching pack. The dogs were soon surrounding them, howling cheerfully at them. In a moment Sir Harry came puffing into view.

"Damn it, Lou! Why don't they ever come to me when I call?" he asked petulantly.

"Papa, it is high time that we returned to the house," his daughter said sternly, ignoring his complaint.

"What? What?" He looked up at the sky, perceiving that it was in fact later than he had realized. "Didn't realize it was so late!" he remarked cheerfully as he turned toward the house. "It will soon be time for dinner. You are staying to sup with us, Lord Geffrey? Good! Come along, your mother will be back and wondering what has happened to us."

"Sir Harry, if I may, could I talk with you as we walk back?" Lord Geffrey asked diffidently.

"And I will see the dogs to the kennels," Louisa added.

As Sir Harry sputtered, "What? What?" she whistled the milling dogs into order and took them down another path toward their quarters, and Lord Geffrey firmly took the bewildered parent's arm.

By the time Louisa had returned to the house her father was all smiles, her fiance somewhat exhausted by the difficulties of offering a formal offer of marriage to his lady's father while they stumbled through the underbrush. Sir Harry beamed with pleasure, pinched her cheek, and ordered her to go put on her prettiest dress.

Lady Bardoff, soon apprised of the happy event, exclaimed loud and long at her daughter's good fortune, her own surprise and pleasure, and how pleased she was to welcome Lord Geffrey to the family. She began to plan some really splendid parties to celebrate the event.

After dinner there was but one thing to be done to make the accord complete. Louisa took her betrothed by the hand and led him to the great hall. There she stationed him before the tapestries and lit the many candelabra in the room.

"There it is, my lord," she said casually.

"Francis."

"Francis." She dimpled, then added, "I longed to say it at table but lacked the courage."

He smiled at her tenderly, his attention totally diverted from what she had brought him to see. For a moment she gazed back at him, then recalled herself with a start.

"The wallhanging! You haven't looked once at the wallhanging!"

"What does it have to do with anything?" he asked idly, glancing up.

"Everything!"

Above him was a sight he had never expected to see. Carefully stitched into the canvas was a scene of much splendor, an unusual combination of Egyptian, Roman, and imaginative motives. In the middle, a carpet was piled in a tumble, and from it rose a striking, dark-haired woman of vaguely foreign appearance. She was stretching out her arms in a dramatic gesture toward a man in a curious toga.

"Cleopatra's Carpet!" Louisa said in a hushed tone.

"My God!" was all Francis Geffrey could mutter.

Louisa ruined her pose with a giggle. "It is dreadful, isn't it? Mama and the Dowager Lady Howorthy stitched this one together. The other two were mostly done by Lady Howorthy. Mama has always treasured them."

Lord Geffrey was much struck by the other two pictures and was unable to make any suitable comment.

219

"Mama thought that the dowager had left it to her, to round out the group, so to speak. But apparently Lady Howorthy wasn't aware of it and Mama refused to ask for what she thought was hers and was in a taking and . . . Well, that is how the quarrel began."

Her beloved finally managed to speak. "Louisa, you must promise me one thing," he said firmly.

"Yes?"

"You must promise me never to stitch a wall-hanging. Chair covers are unexceptional; after all, when in use they can't be seen. But not wallhangings. You may even replant every square foot of the parks and gardens of my country seat, but *no* wall-hangings!"

"Yes dear," Louisa promised demurely, her eyes sparkling wickedly.

"I couldn't bear to live with it," he explained with simple dignity. Then catching sight of the expression on her face, he pulled her roughly into his arms and kissed her.

XX

The announcement of the engagement of Louisa Bardoff to Lord Geffrey was met with surprise and some cynicism. Many people, Mr. Scropes among them, failed to see how such a plain young lady could manage to run through so many fiancés in one Season. When the Dowager Countess of Sitwell announced a ball, the last and grandest of the Season, in honor of the betrothal, people who had left Town for the country found it worth their while to return. Driven by curiosity, they opened up their town houses or moved into hotels, prepared to be richly entertained by the coming event.

They were even more surprised when they arrived at the ball. At the head of the receiving line was Miss Bardoff, resplendent in a vivid blue gown of silk that set off her eyes and her new attractive figure to advantage. She greeted her many guests with a dignity that had always been there, but was only now being appreciated by many. More than one older guest murmured on the resemblance to her famous ancestress, the first Louisa, and the cynical and worldly were suitably impressed. The Dowager Lady Geffrey stood by, a look of pride on her face, and some were so uncharitable as to call her obvious complaisance smugness. No, Francis Geffrey had not taken leave of his senses.

How in the world he would have known that his bride would be so stunning was a matter of some conjecture. Mr. Scropes, malicious as ever, spread the tale that he had inspected her first on several visits to Bardoff Hall before making a formal offer. Others, chagrined that they had lacked the foresight to realize that the puppy fat would melt away to reveal a perfect figure and lovely face, lent him their attention. Freddy Witherspoon could not see what the fuss was all about. After all, it was still the same Louisa, dressed a bit differently, it was true, but as gay as ever. If Lord Geffrey ever felt a pang of jealousy, it was toward this young man. His sincere admiration of Louisa, both old and new, made far more of an impression on that young lady than all the flowery compliments she was now receiving.

During a waltz later in the evening, he seized the opportunity to tease her.

"Do you realize that I am being credited by some as a wizard of sorts? However did I manage to get in my offer before everyone else discovered you?"

"You got in your offer without even noticing that there had been a change!" she laughed back. "When I think of that dress I was wearing! How did you have the nerve to offer for such a shabby creature?"

"You know that I proposed for the sole purpose of being one step ahead of the others, Mr. Scropes in particular. My goal is to discomfort them to the utmost."

"Mr. Scropes would see it that way!"

"I merely wanted to claim the Season's greatest beauty before you had a chance to look around and before they had a chance to see you," he said loftily.

"A social coup!"

"Exactly."

"I shall have to gain back all that weight to prove them wrong," she said determinedly.

"If it would make you happy, love, please do," he said adoringly.

"You are supposed to protest, sir, and not take my threats so lightly!" she scolded.

"I would have to put up the blunt for a new wardrobe again," he murmured appreciatively. "I hadn't thought of that."

"Definitely! No matter what my figure is, I refuse

to wear any more of those flounces and ruffles! That must be made clear from the beginning!"

"Quite." He paused, a thoughtful look on his face. "But perhaps you could just remove them from the old dresses?"

"Francis!"

"Quite," he grinned, and he spun her around the floor with a laugh.